The Fifth Di...

March 2021

Features

Short Stories

Flash Fiction

Poetry

*

THE STAFF OF THE FIFTH DI...:

EDITOR: Tyree Campbell
WEBMASTER: H David Blalock

Cover art "In the Belly of the Beast" by Laura Givens
Cover design by Laura Givens

Vol. II, No.1   March 2021

A Little Help, Please

In the world of the small indie press we fight a never-ending battle for attention to our work, as writers and in publishing. Here's an example: big publishers [you know who they are] have gobs of $$$ that they can devote to advertising and marketing. Here at Hiraeth Publishing, our advertising budget consists of the deposits for whatever soda bottles and aluminum cans we can find alongside the highways. Anti-littering laws make our task even more difficult . . . ☺

That's where YOU come in. YOU are our best promoter. YOU are the one who can tell others about us. Just send 'em to our website, tell them about our store. That's all. Just that.

Of course, we don't mind if you talk us up. We're pretty good, you know. We have some award-winning and award-nominated writers and artists, plus other voices well-deserving to be heard [not everyone wins awards, right?] but our publications are read-worthy nevertheless.

That number once again is:

www.hiraethsffh.com

Friend us on Facebook at Hiraeth Publishing
Follow us on Twitter at @HiraethPublish1

TYREE
CAMPBELL

BECOMING
JADE

Annae (real name Maryjade) is an assassin sent to Deege, a forested world, to kill a plant and bring back the druzy who carries it. Druzies resemble young girls, but seem to have no life and no purpose but to act as transportation to the plants. In the process, Annae loses contact with her own spacecraft and is marooned on the world.

The man who hired Annae for this task is also responsible for the death of Annae's twin sister. Annae has accepted this contract because it presents an opportunity to kill the killer. However, the loss of the twin has crippled Annae. She is virtually unable to communicate with anyone, except in the course of negotiating her contracts. She has taken to talking with the memory of her dead sister, and with no one else.

Now, marooned on Deege, she must find a way to break out of her isolation and communicate with the druzies, and with a strange young woman who cannot speak, or she will be compelled to remain on this world forever.

https://www.hiraethsffh.com/product-page/becoming-jade-by-tyree-campbell

What???
No subscription to
The Fifth Di...??

We can fix that . . .

The Fifth Di... is a quarterly publication, released each year in March, June, September, and December. It contains science fiction, fantasy, and some dark fiction short stories, poems, articles, reviews, and art. We offer one- and two-year subscriptions. Go to the link below and order. Simple.

https://www.hiraethsffh.com/product-page/fifth-di

And remember: a subscription makes a great gift, for a holiday or birthday or any time of the year!

FEATURED STORY:

What if it were a marathon dance to the death? What if you danced with her as if it were the last time?

Danse Macabre Days
Brandon Kingdollar

"Alright, kids, it's seven o'clock. You all know what that means!" yelled Jack from the back bar, where he'd been pouring beers for high schoolers all night.

It was December 31st, 1979. When I tell you Magic Jack's Honk Tonk Diner was hopping that night, it was shaking to the beat—I mean it was happening. His was a place where you could rock and roll all night, forget your troubles, just grab your mama and swing her around the floor like the party would never stop. Maybe, if everybody did their part, it didn't have to.

The smell of grease kissed you on the mouth the moment you slammed open those friendly double doors, and it was the greatest feeling in the world.

I'd spent many nights at Jack's throughout high school, but this one was different, a night of mourning. The diner was to close with the New Year. We were giving her our best send-off, a regular Viking funeral. For me, it was one ending too many.

Sitting at the barstool next to mine was my best girl, Cindy Gallagher. It was our senior year, time to kiss the rockstar dream goodbye. I was going off to college—first in my family to earn that distinction—the University of Toledo, about five hundred miles away.

I hadn't told her.

Guess I thought I could protect her. Maybe I figured we could just dance the truth away; if we had enough fun, if we rocked hard enough, I could stick around. I loved that girl.

The jukebox died out like an orchestra dimming for its honored guest. We all had a degree of reverence for Jack, and I swear to God, it wasn't just because he let us drink all we wanted at his fine establishment. He was an icon, impossibly old and impossibly wrinkled and yet still cooler than a Frigidaire. Drove a '58 Chevy Bel Air everywhere he went, and that shit was as cherry as the day it rolled off the assembly line. Aside from when he cruised town in that beauty, we never really saw him out of the diner. He was a myth and you just had to make a pilgrimage to Magic Jack's to see him for yourself.

"I've got a special treat for all you kids tonight: the diner ain't closing 'til morning!" He paused, gestured, and summoned a belated cheer already slurred by the spirits of the night. "We're gonna have ourselves a dance marathon, gonna dance our way into the 1980s! If you sit, you're out. If you fall over drunk, you're out. If you stop moving or piss or do anything besides hop to the beat and dance the night away, you're out."

"And what does the winner get?" called out one of my old buddies, Alex Armstead, already in a drunken stupor.

Behind his bar, Magic Jack smiled, a thin sliver of a smile like he was about to con you out of your life savings. The kind of smile that glints like moonlight and turns you to stone until it's off the offender's face and out of your memory.

"You get one wish."

The diner erupted with laughter. Jack was a regular comedian, cracked everybody up for miles from his seat at the back of the bar. He didn't join us this time. The laughter died when we realized Jack intended the remark to be serious.

"So we could wish for your Chevy?" asked Cindy, stifling a giggle.

"Yes, of course," he indulged.

Alex chimed in: "We could wish for the keys to the diner?"

"Sure, I don't see why not," Jack allowed.

"We could wish for a lifetime of free beer?" asked a twenty-year-old senior.

8

"You can wish for any damned thing you want! That's why they call it a wish, numbnuts!" he snarled. Jack practically leapt at the kid, who fell back in his barstool, shattering his pitcher of beer. We all shared a laugh at his expense. "If you're in, stick around. If you're out, do me a favor and get the hell out of my bar."

Nobody did so much as cough. When I say the room was quiet, it was still as a headstone—I mean, it was dead in there. I figured some of the lightweights or out-of-towners would scramble for the door, start up their cruisers, and drive the hell right out of Dodge, but nobody took the bait. All they saw was an old man who'd sampled too much of his own supply. If they were in a dive like this on New Year's, they probably didn't have anywhere else to go.

A shiver rattled through Cindy as though she suddenly realized it was winter beyond those sleek double doors. I put an arm around her, as you do, and pulled her close to me. Gave her a kiss on the cheek (or that was the idea, but I ended up planting it in the vicinity of her temple), but when I looked into her eyes, she didn't even consider the possibility of leaving Jack's. He liked screwing with kids, and drunk kids were the most fun to play jokes on. I think we all just assumed this was another one of those.

"That's what I like to hear. In about a minute, I'm gonna start this juke up again, and you'd all better be on that dancefloor when I do. If you ain't, you're out. If you stop moving, you're—ah shit, you get the point, you ain't idiots." We stood there gawking, like teenagers caught getting fresh out in the old barn. "Well? Go on then! Don't just stand there—dance!"

Everybody shuffled out to the varnished wood and got ready to cut a rug. I don't think any of us really understood what we were getting into—none of us were really the dance marathon type, you dig? We were all teenagers whose only dancing experience consisted of awkwardly shuffling with the object of our affection at the odd sock hop.

Well, except for Cindy and I. Back at the Sadie Hawkins, our first date, we'd been the brightest stars of that dying galaxy, maybe because we weren't afraid to

9

spin each other around. I was mostly too busy staring at her to focus on what the rest of my body was doing, though. But that's neither here nor there.

What you've gotta understand about a dance marathon —it's a test of endurance, not skill, not God-given talent. We were farmboys and farmgirls, so we had that in spades —but little else.

"Let's get out there, loverboy," she suggested, giving me a look that suggested there might be some extracurricular dancing after the main event if I played my cards right. It was a smoky look, gone as soon as you knew it was there. If I'd won the marathon right then and there, I think I would've wished to stay in that moment with her forever.

The moment we were in the dancefloor's clutches, Jack pounded his fist against the side of the jukebox like he was on Happy Days, banged on his cowbell, and we were off.

The first song was "Crocodile Rock" by Elton John, and looking back, I think it encapsulated the whole night. Cindy and I skipped to that beat, and it was like the Sadie Hawkins dance all over again—I couldn't tear my eyes from hers. At that dance, though, she'd kept looking away, as though if she met my gaze, I'd put a spell on her.

This time, her eyes—bright and sparkling blue, full of young hope—never shied away from mine. We'd had a lot of practice since that dance last September, I guess.

"Got some moves on you, Reeves," she said as we spun and we twirled, as the record machine hopped and bopped in its corner, as Magic Jack sat there in the corner laughing at some long-forgotten joke only he understood.

"You would know," I said right back. Like John and his Crocodile Rock, we really thought it would last. Something wrenched in my gut as I imagined my Mustang flush with boxes on its way to Ohio, Cindy watching from her window with a face that was a mask of tears. I had to get out of here; I had to stay. And only the man on the jukebox understood my dilemma.

Somebody clapped me on the shoulder, probably Alex, as if to congratulate me on the girl I'd lucked into. She was a beautiful, vibrant flower and I was going to crush her to dust in my hand without even warning her. All at once, the song on the juke didn't seem so important. All at once, my stomach was churning, and I just had to tell her, had to tell her. I'd pull her off the floor and confess. Didn't matter if we were out of Jack's stupid contest—I needed to warn her of the pain because I loved her more than anyone else in the world.

Her attention was on Brittany Lark, who was having something of an episode at the center of the dance floor. Whole pitcher of beer in her hand from her table. We watched that amber poison rock back and forth as she tottered, as she slurred. All we gave her was a wide berth and scandalized looks. No help. No sympathy. Even Cindy had nothing but pity to offer.

I tapped her on the shoulder: "Hey, Cin," I said, but as she turned, the boozed-up girl in the sparkling red dress stole the show. She swooned and fell to the wooden floor with a savage thump, shattering the mug and spilling beer across the boards.

Nobody stopped dancing, and I can't tell you why. Girl could have split her head open, but we all just kept dancing, secure in our belief that she'd pop right back up.

"You're out," called Magic Jack from the rear of the room, disinterested. It was a callous remark for a girl who could have been concussed—but that was the least of her worries.

We watched, transfixed in collective horror, as the sister we'd shared for four years writhed in pain on that magical dancefloor. She opened her mouth to scream, but the sound never came. Brittany Lark melted into a pile of dust beneath our stomping feet. Baffled terror swam in her eyes. She'd never know her fate; the rest of us were cursed with that knowledge.

There came one horrible moment between songs where we contemplated the stakes of the game. One girl had entered this dancefloor full of hopes and dreams and now she would never leave it, nothing but a river of dust between the cracks in the floor.

Then, the jukebox started back up, and we all kept grooving because it was dance or die, baby, and we all had a strong preference for the former. From the juke came a clunking, skittering sound and before we could note where the girl had fallen on the floor, Elton John began to sing "Crocodile Rock" once more. Record skip. Jack offered a creaking cackle.

Cindy started to shake, her eyes wide with fear, still not comprehending how somebody could be here one second and not be the next, only dust to signify they'd ever been alive. To my right was a flurry of movement. I whirled, spinning Cindy with me. She let out a yelp of surprise.

I caught a glimpse of a couple I knew, but I didn't know their names. The ones you share good times with that you forget the moment you toss your cap into the air. Maybe you half-remember a beer-fueled night decades later, but it's gone as quick as it comes. Those two were ephemeral, the guy with his greasy black hair and leather jacket, the girl with shaggy blonde hair and a schoolgirl smile. He looked like Travolta. I guess they could've been Danny and Sandy.

The glimpse was all I caught. Danny and his best girl ran in blind terror from the center of the dancefloor in the direction of the door. He only managed one step past the threshold.

"You're out!" Jack snarled again, just having the time of his life. Panic seized Danny, and I could see the plea forming on his lips as the invisible barrier where wooden boards met linoleum vaporized him. It cut through his good looks like a laser, first erasing the skin—giving us a good look at the ivory white of his bones, of his skull—before turning that to ash as well.

Sandy's shrill shriek shattered beer glasses that night. Her case was all the more tragic, because she watched him die and tried so hard to catch herself, skittered right to the edge of that wooden floor. For a moment, we thought she was going to make it. The girl swayed forward and backward, tipsy from the beers Jack had been supplying, and in the end she had just a shred too much of forward momentum. The girl toppled forward, but never found the ground. Left behind only her best dancing shoes, which remained safely on the sanctified wooden boards.

12

As my feet kept moving to the piano and the guitar, as I swung Cindy this way and that, I reflected on one comforting fact: Danny and Sandy went together. They at least had that.

I thought Cindy would cry, could see tears on the horizon of her eyes, so I did the only thing I could think of to still her: I kissed her on the lips. She clung to me tightly, as though some riptide would tear us apart. We slowed, realized that we'd need to pace ourselves, but kept moving from one foot to another. Forced to dance on the mass grave.

"Crocodile Rock" started for the third time, and that's when the time started to melt together. Maybe I was drunk, maybe I was in shock, maybe it was the fact that the jukebox wouldn't stop playing that damned song. There'd been... oh, maybe forty of us to start, I'm not sure if that's too high or too low, but an hour later (or a minute or a year; who could tell?), that number was halved. Cindy closed her eyes whenever Jack spoke. I was haunted on her behalf.

"I want to go home," she said to me in one of the lulls between songs, and it tore my heart in two. I'd brought her here. I'd gotten her drunk. Her fate was my fault alone.

Why did we have to die? Why couldn't we be young forever?

My friends, my classmates left this world one by one. It wasn't terror in their eyes—it was disbelief. We were invincible. The death of our dreams hurt more than that of our bodies. I think I preferred seeing terror, disbelief to acceptance, acceptance that the great roulette wheel left us penniless, acceptance that dreams die.

The jughead who was set on wishing for Jack's whole beer supply (Tommy McGrady, his name was, and we spoke it like a plague) knocked into the captain of the football team, and trapped him in his high school days. Not before the captain got a fistful of Tommy's shirt and dragged him to hell, though, nothing but a tortured wail marking their exit from our world.

By then, we were fifteen.

"Why are you doing this to us?" asked Alex, indignant. It was a good question, and I wondered why none of us had asked it before. Too busy fighting for our lives, I suppose. "You want to teach us a lesson or something, that your game? Or do you just hate kids?"

Jack strode to the floor from the back bar. There was good humor on the shark's face.

"Did you really expect to live forever?"

I don't know if it was courage or suicide, but I respected the hell out of it: Alex rushed the old man and swung a meaty fist at his head. The bones crunched in Jack's timeless face. He'd convinced us he was a friend. Smiled and poured us beers. Alex's punch gave us life.

I respected him too much to look away. The killing force kissed his fist first, vaporized it, and crept up his arm, consuming the rest of his body. It was a sickening thing, watching your best friend die. I thought back to sneaking out to the trainyard and chugging beers with Alex, breaking bottles with Alex, playing basketball in the driveway with Alex. Friendships like that were built to last. You were never supposed to lose them, not after high school, not ever.

Nothing prepared you for watching your best friend die.

As he vanished from the face of the earth, good old Alex Armstead—grinning, laughing, joking Alex—flashed a smile at me, bigger and brighter than I'd ever seen. It was a doofus smile: *Look at the mess we've gotten into.* I'd never forget that Alex went down smiling.

I wasn't sure if it was the delirium of the night, or the beer going to my head, but I swear that grin hung in the air for a moment after Alex left our world. Like the damned Cheshire Cat.

Magic Jack sprung back up, but he was human after that sock to the jaw. He rubbed at it, almost in shock. I could tell he wanted to do something for that slight, but it was difficult to take vengeance on a dead man. Instead, he just cranked the juke louder.

My gaze found Cindy as Elton John shook the room. We wanted to comfort each other, make it alright, but we found no words. Instead, I held her tighter and she reciprocated. Our legs were getting so very tired. Our feet

14

were cratered with oozing blisters. I wondered if it might be better to give in. Let the creeping waves take us. Go together like Danny and Sandy had.

If she thought the same thing, she was too scared to voice it. We were kids. Death was never real to us before that night, and we wouldn't live to pass along the warning that it was.

In the end, we kept dancing. I don't know if it was the hypnosis of the lights or that idiotic certainty that we really were invincible, even as our friends fell dead beside us, but we kept dancing. What choice did we have? We were hostage to the music.

Days passed, months passed, years passed; it became impossible to tell. Was it 1980? Was it 2000? Time had no meaning in Magic Jack's any more than it did in a prison cell or a sinking ship. Minutes turned to hours and time stretched out forever when you needed it most.

Eventually (and I can't say how long this was the case before I noticed; after Alex, I couldn't make myself watch the others) Cindy and I were the only ones left. Magic Jack circled the dancefloor, eying us like chum, waiting for one of us to finally drop from exhaustion. In a horrible mockery of the Sadie Hawkins dance, I couldn't take my eyes off Cindy, sweet Cindy, innocent Cindy. Two circling stars now locked in an endless death spiral.

I let go of her but kept moving.

"Cin, I love you so much, I want you to know that. But I brought you here. I'm taking the fall, kid. You've got a future. I won't be the one to end it."

I drifted towards the edge of the dance floor, spinning towards that event horizon. It wouldn't hurt. If I didn't think about it—if I never left her enchanting eyes—it wouldn't hurt.

I tried to believe that.

"I begged you to bring me," she reminded me, and yeah, I'd conveniently forgotten that fact. "I'm the one who asked for trouble. Ted, you're the one with a future. Your mom showed me the letter from the University of Toledo. I was just going to spin my wheels after you left. I'm not a college girl, I'm barely a high school girl. If anybody should go, it's me."

15

"Hey, lovebirds, as much as I enjoy the spectacle, let's wrap this up. Midnight looms," said Jack, like he would turn into a pumpkin at the fated hour. Cindy and I glared, silencing him.

"I ain't asking, Cindy. It's not right for me to let you die. It's going to be me, and that's final." I thought for a moment. "Besides, if I walked out of here, your daddy would kill me himself. You at least have a shot." It was only a half-joke. I didn't have the heart for a full one.

"Fine," she said, and she left it at that and a stifled whimper. It was the same as a year ago—she couldn't meet my gaze. "Just... will you do me one thing?"

"Anything."

"Kiss me. For the last time."

I walked to her, for one moment out of the clutches of that terrible black hole that lurks in all our futures. I slipped an arm around her waist, lost myself in the ocean of her gaze. Remembered our first kiss, at the Sadie Hawkins, where we'd bumped noses before finally hitting the target. She'd tasted like cherries, maybe it was her lipstick. We were awkward then and we were confident now. It was a deep kiss, one with awful finality, one that I never wanted to pull away from. My soul flowed into her as I stepped into my grave. Love never died.

While I was still enraptured by her kiss, her eyes, her stunning beauty, she threw herself to the floor. I didn't have time to cry out, didn't even have time to breathe. Her eyes apologized while her mouth conveyed her final message: "I love you."

True high school sweethearts were never supposed to lose each other. We were soulmates lucky enough to find each other this early in life and we'd been punished for it. Losing friends was harrowing. Losing love was worse than losing life itself. It should have been me.

In one moment, she was my entire world; in the next, she was dust.

"You're out."

The jukebox died. I fell to my knees, choking out sobs that only somebody who'd forgotten how to cry could produce, tortured weeping that always seemed to miss the mark. Tears streaked my face. An awful, booming clock chimed tonelessly. Happy New Year.

Magic Jack clapped me on the back, and my skin wanted to flee from his fingers.

"Congrats, boy! It's you! You get the wish!"

I wanted to wish death on him, but his eyes begged for that mercy. I wouldn't supply it.

It was strange being able to think. The Crocodile Rock had died with Cindy and the diner was morbidly still. The obvious answer was to wish everyone back to life, but that would take us back to square one. I felt like I was owed something after this ordeal. Besides, the horrors of that night were only a preview of what would come. I'd still lose all of those friends, and someday, I'd lose Cindy. It would just be slower, more painful. Time made fools of us all.

I never wanted to lose my friends, my love. I wanted the rockstar dream to live forever.

I turned to Jack. The man had alligator eyes. I didn't understand how I'd never noticed them before. If he didn't owe the wish, he would have eaten me then and there.

"I wish the 70s would never end."

"Wish granted," said Magic Jack, still a sneer on his face. He slammed a fist into the jukebox and sparks of every color shot into the air. My vision bleared to nothing.

Time could never touch us.

***

That beautiful aroma of grease kissed me before anything else. A waitress bustled by, and a hand waved in front of my face.

"Hey, space cadet, did you hear me? I said, let's get out there, loverboy." Cindy melted me with a smile as she pulled me out to the dancefloor.

Jack punched the jukebox to life and flashed a knowing smile.

I held onto Cindy. I never wanted the night to end.

Customer Complaint
Andrew Jensen

"Do I need a lawyer? I haven't done anything wrong, you know." The tiny, wiry woman in overalls glared at the large officer seated across from her.

"You're only here to make a statement," came the professionally calming reply. "It's standard procedure. You're welcome to call a lawyer, if you like. It'll take longer, though."

The woman thought for a moment, then nodded abruptly. "Okay, as long as I'm just making a statement. None of this is my fault."

"My name is Rita Ginsberg. I'm a professional contractor and a master carpenter. I mostly do renovations. That's what I did for this family."

The officer interrupted: "Mostly renovations? Are new homes too much for you?"

Rita scowled. "You're a weekend carpenter, aren't you? Those workshops at *Home Nursery* don't teach you everything. I *could* work new construction, but I like renos better. It's more challenging, and I enjoy blending woods, getting old and new to work together in an attractive way. It's more of an art. When you grow the house from the ground up, there's no real challenge."

"But how do you make the new wood match the old? I looked at it, and I can tell that it's an addition." The officer was scowling back.

"What's the point of matching? Everyone says they want nice hardwood floors, but no one wants to wait for them. With a reno, the family is still in the house, so you have to graft in the new wood and get it to grow quickly. Soft woods are faster, and easier to shape. If you choose well, the contrast is stunningly beautiful. I take pride in my work."

The officer grunted, unconvinced. "Are all your licenses in order? Do you have the necessary permits?"

Rita's voice grew frosty. "I have all the forms. I'm a

professional. Here, I brought them. See? They signed the release saying no one had any allergies to the material I was using. How was I supposed to know they'd react?"

The officer scanned through the official documents. "These don't prove much. Everyone knows that contractors cut corners all the time."

Rita nearly exploded. "You've been watching *Big Dan's Reno Rescue*, haven't you? That guy's such a jerk, going around and tearing down other people's work. It's unethical, publicly denouncing other hard-working contractors on his 'reality show,' and acting like some kind of saviour. I've registered formal complaints against him with the Woodworker's Guild. Not that *they* did anything. It's an old boys club.

"He's a dinosaur, always on camera in his undershirt, so everyone can admire his muscles. Every hair is always perfectly in place. It's unnatural! He must think he's God's Gift or something. He might as well be a stone mason or a brick layer."

The officer glanced up sharply. "What's the problem with stone masons and brick layers?"

Rita's face reddened. "Uh, nothing. Nothing at all. I have total respect for those trades. But stones and bricks are dead. Wood is alive. It's wonderful to work with."

The officer cleared his throat. "Ms. Ginsberg, are you a member of SOER?"

Rita shrugged. "No. I've never heard of it. Isn't it French for 'sister' or something? I don't belong to any women's groups."

"SOER stands for the Society of Old Earth Re-enactors."

Rita gasped. "You think I'm a terrorist? No way! Do you know what they do? Their so-called 'carpenters' use saws, and nails, and screws! Screws! Murderers! My great-grandparents didn't risk everything to terraform this planet just so we could slip back into barbarism. Old Earth is a mess, and these idiots want to go back to *those* ways? They're Eco-terrorists, that's what they are. You know, I bet they're behind this."

The officer smirked. "What makes you think that? I thought you'd never heard of them."

Rita took a deep breath, and let it out slowly. "I've never heard their name before. But all these Old-Earth types are extremists and terrorists. This is *just* the kind of trouble they'd make, isn't it? Why don't you ask them?"

"I'll be speaking to them, don't worry. But I want to gather basic information first. As you pointed out, *I'm* not a professional carpenter. You can help me understand how all this might have happened. Do you mind if I ask some questions about the renovation process?"

Rita leaned back, looking calmer, but still wary. "I suppose. What do you want to know?"

"First of all, those 'terrorists,' as you call them, claim that their saws and screws are ancient and time-honored methods of construction. Some of them also object to the use of Genetically Modified Organisms that allow for fast growth. Don't you have any concerns about that?"

Rita sighed. "This is pretty basic stuff, you know. Anyone could get it off the net."

The officer smiled insincerely. "Humor me. You can't trust a lot of what you read there. I'd rather hear it from a *professional*."

"Okay. First of all, I don't care how time-honored something is: if it's wrong, it's wrong. Working with living wood is always better than killing a plant to make something.

"Secondly, genetic modification is mostly used for the rapid growth of hardwoods. You know, like the oak for the original construction. Softer woods grow faster naturally. All you need are some enhanced hormone formulas to do the work. 'Be Nice, Don't Splice.'"

The officer pointedly ignored the familiar slogan. "Is this hormone a restricted substance? Can just anyone buy it?"

"Anyone can buy a mild version of it, but they shouldn't use it on their vegetables. It's not safe to eat. Carpenters use a stronger concentration. That stuff'll work on any soft wood you give me. With that, I can make any shape you want." Rita paused, saw that her audience looked unimpressed, and added: "I'm licensed to use it." Rita scrolled to one of the documents.

The officer glanced at it, and then consulted some

notes. "You used vines as part of the renovation. Vines aren't strong, are they? Is that standard practice?"

Rita relaxed more. "You can't use vines for load bearing structures, but they make great decorative trim. They're flexible, and they can be accelerated into really fast, ornate growth. You can even do some kinds of furniture if you have the skills. That's what I did for this family. They wanted a sauna addition. Of course, most of their house is oak. It's solid, and they've kept it well watered and fed."

The officer interrupted again. "Oak? But it says here that you used cedar."

"Like I said, people want fast results. Oak is slow-growing, and I avoid GMOs. Cedar is ideal for a sauna, so I grafted it on for most of the addition: the floor, walls and ceiling. I wanted a nice decorative alternative for the benches, so I went for ivy vines. I take great pride in choosing the best wood for the job."

"But you said making vine furniture is harder. Why not use some other wood?"

Rita shook her head impatiently. "This isn't just some cheap shack I'm making. I take pride in my designs. Sometimes I'll choose a shrub, like holly, for decorative furniture: it gives a really attractive effect, with natural edges to contrast with all the organic curves. I love it for mirror frames and coat racks. But it's way too spiky for a bench, especially in a sauna. Think about it: it's not something you'd want to sit on, is it?

"Ivy has a long tradition with buildings, even stone ones. It's attractive and it can be woven into a great bench. This sauna was some of my best work. I don't understand why they're complaining."

The officer gave Rita a piece of paper. "Forensics has given us this report on the bench. Do you have any comment?"

Rita scowled again as she read through the document. "No, no. This can't be! This is just *wrong!*"

The officer smirked. "So you deny that this is the wood you used?"

Rita had gone pale. "Is this for real?"

The officer tapped the paper. "Our biologists have confirmed it. It comes from Old Earth, and has *never* been seen here before. *You're* the 'professional.' *You* 'take pride' in choosing your own materials. Now answer the question: is this the wood you used?"

As Rita was led away in handcuffs, she twisted uselessly between the huge, implacable guards escorting her to the cells. "I want a lawyer! Talk to my supplier! I've been hacked! I swear, I've never even heard of *poison* ivy!"

Gaia
Maureen Bowden

You fracked:
cracked my bones.
My moans fill your ears.
You spill your bladder on the beach,
reach the promenade and run,
as my spasm wracks and rends
sea walls,
Bingo halls,
shopping malls.
My seizure sends the wave
across your concrete pavements,
invades your city's arteries
as you invaded mine.
You cry for pity.
Where was yours for me?

Wipeout
Steve DuBois

FIRST CONSTRUCTIVE

"We, as the negative team in this debate, propose that you exterminate the human race. The chief flaw in the affirmative team's policy proposal lies not in the mechanics of how it protects people, but in the assumption that people should be protected. In your notes, judges, please label our overall argument: Wipeout. It is an overarching strategy with several interlocking components. Amit and I believe that you will find that the pieces fit."

The debate final is underway, the arguments unraveling under flickering fluorescent lights, and Connor's shirt sleeve is unraveling with them. His clothing is threadbare, the sleeves of the suit he outgrew two years ago riding up his forearms, revealing a frayed left cuff, a missing button. Whenever his hands are left idle, they return to the cuff, picking and plucking nervously. It's amazing, over time, how the wear accumulates, how much thoughtless damage is done.

The boy himself is gawky and angular, addicted to argument. He hunches over the desk, battered laptop open before him, hitching in quick double-breaths between sentences, spewing facts and spittle. Connor is awkward, and he is unkempt almost to the point of being anti-kempt. But Connor is a tactician. You've yet to even open your mouth, and Connor already knows what you're going to say and why you're wrong.

Beside him, Amit. Amit is tiny and brown, his necktie impeccably knotted by his mother that morning, and there is no unkindness in him. Amit can speak at three hundred and thirty words per minute without a stumble or a bobble. Amit skipped two grades and posted a 36 ACT at age fourteen. Amit can't ask a girl out on a date without his throat swelling shut from pure terror. But stick an equation in front of him or an argumentative brief in his hand, and Amit becomes a machine.

The room contains a triumvirate of adult judges and a plethora of adolescent spectators and the clacking and rattling of fingers on keyboards and the breathless, rapid-fire drone of Connor's voice. And the room contains the surprised expressions on the faces of their opponents, Maggie and Amanda, and the quizzical glance between them, as Connor drops the bomb.

SECOND CONSTRUCTIVE

"Adoption of the affirmative's policy will result in several disadvantages, the first of which you may label Vacuum Metastability. In Subpoint A we note that the affirmative prevents a nuclear war. This, of course, is *their* claim. You may have found their reasoning specious when they presented it, but you shouldn't hold it against them. It's just the way things work in modern high school debate. Judges are expected to weigh the benefits and the drawbacks of the affirmative's proposal. In search of the biggest impact to weigh, both teams inevitably race towards apocalypse. We will not dispute their claim; we concede it. In fact, we will double down on their behalf: as this evidence from Professor Schell in 1994 demonstrates, the war they prevent would inevitably result in human extinction.

And that's the problem. Our Subpoint B points to mankind's continual and unwise experimentation with particle colliders. As Dr. Ammerman demonstrates in this evidence from 2014, our curiosity will ultimately kill us, as particle collisions create microscopic black holes with the capacity to suck in our entire solar system. Worse still, as Till in '08 shows, is the probability that experiments of this sort could cause the collapse of the universe from a false to a true vacuum state—creating a *new* universe with its own set of physical laws, expanding outwards from a fixed point at the speed of light.

Sometimes the best way of disproving an argument is to take its premises seriously. Amit and I demonstrate

24

that humanity must always seek to prove its intelligence, and that this urge to prove ourselves will prove the universe's undoing—unless we undo ourselves first. We need the nuclear war, judges. We need the extinction of the human race to save the universe. You must reject the affirmative, judges. You must negate."

The first day Connor wore a suit was the worst day of Connor's life. Ever since, putting on a tie has triggered a psychosomatic reaction, a gnawing in his stomach accompanied by a cold, sour sweat and a feeling of impending doom. He has taught himself to channel it all, to burn it as fuel, and now Connor's laptop and his mouth are roaring wide open, and the data pours forth, and from it, Connor knits a narrative of apocalypse. Vacuum Metastability first, and then four more disadvantages to the affirmative plan as well as a critique of the affirmative's philosophy: a smorgasbord of anti-human arguments from which each judge may select her personal favorite. Things fall apart, by Connor's design; the center cannot hold, he will not let it. Maggie and Amanda, at the desk across the room, ensconced behind laptops of their own, stare slack-jawed as Connor rhetorically exterminates the human species. They had carefully crafted a proposal to ameliorate American poverty, had meticulously researched its merits, had prepared, or so they thought, against all possible objections. But then, alas, they claimed to prevent nuclear war. Connor and Amit have seized the opportunity, have taken them to a place they were unprepared to go. Amanda and Maggie had assumed that the value of human life was common ground. Connor has ripped that ground from beneath their feet, and they plummet, grasping for reasons and for the right words.

The words do not come. Connor wipes out humanity and wins. Connor and Amit soak up the applause of the crowd and the adulation of their debate coach. Connor basks in the admiring glow of Ambriel's gaze. Fragrant Ambriel, with her perfect face, her showy figure, her formidable mind, her fashionable hyphenate of a surname. Connor knows he can never hope to approach her either competitively or socially. On most Saturdays she'd have swept the field clean—but as luck would have it, this weekend, she and her partner stumbled in quarterfinals, and Connor and Amit were there to fill the void.

The day is theirs, as is the first-place trophy—plastic and wood veneer, columns and platforms ascending, crowned by a gilt figurine of a dapper teen, right arm extended in a sweeping gesture, left arm resting lightly atop a lectern. The figure is a fraud, a throwback to a bygone era in which debaters were rhetorical artists as opposed to industrial information processors. *Pretty*, Connor thinks, observing the figurine's posture, *but not realistic*. He can't imagine why any debater would choose such a bizarre stance.

THIRD CONSTRUCTIVE

"The second disadvantage to the affirmative team's proposal is Nanotechnology. Consider first Subpoint A: the affirmative team's plan will prevent a nuclear war, and the ensuing human extinction. In Subpoint B, we note that continued human survival ensures the development of nanoreplicators. Dr. Drexler explained in 1990 that these microscopic machines will disassemble molecules to make new, more useful molecules out of them, in order to build more replicators, in order to make still more molecules. And the impact, in Subpoint C: nanoreplicators will unravel the universe. Smith in 2012: The off switch fails. The replicators start making more of themselves, and they don't stop. The mindless machines turn upon their creators, disassembling us, disassembling Earth, spreading out in a cloud. The solar system, the stellar cluster, the galaxy, dissolve into grey goo. The machines are all.

One single change in the program is all it takes. One single unit can make all the difference. Shut down the program, judges, by shutting down the programmers. Bring on the apocalypse! You must negate."

Connor is leaving the building, trophy under his arm, when he is approached by one of the judges from the final

26

round, probably somebody's mom. He does not know her, which is unusual; debate is a closed community, and the usual adjudicators are former competitors. Seeing her on the finals panel, Connor and Amit resolved themselves to ignore her in favor of the two younger judges, but she surprised them by giving every appearance of being able to follow, and even appreciate, their rapid speech and coldhearted impact calculus. Connor looks at her and cannot think how to describe her; her face registers as undefined, a mathematical average of all faces.

She greets Connor, offers him a vague attempt at a smile. Her eyes, he notices, are a truly strange shade of hazel, almost gold. She stares at him a moment longer. He stops noticing. She remarks upon his tactics in the round. An interesting argument, she says, but can it be that he truly believes it? Connor reflects on the question. Well...sure, he replies. He's not lying. Any debater, to sell an argument with full conviction, must first sell themselves on its virtues. He *did*, at the moment of advocacy, believe the argument to be true.

The woman offers Connor that strange smile again, and leans in close. He leans in as well. She turns to him, grips him firmly by the collar, and whispers thirteen words in his ear. Ten of the words would be familiar to any eight-year-old. The eleventh is more advanced. The twelfth is a word Connor has never heard before, and the thirteenth is, perhaps, not a word at all; Connor can't fathom what part of speech it might be, or even how a human tongue could shape the syllables. The words fit together imperfectly. They express a thought, but they are not quite a sentence.

As he sifts through the thirteen words, over and over again, in his head, on his walk to his beaten-up Oldsmobile, on the ride home to the carefully maintained double-wide he shares with his father, who is working another double shift and won't be home for hours, won't be home for dinner, won't see Connor at all that night, won't know of his great victory until its savor has faded, until Connor is uninterested in discussing it—as Connor spins and flips the words in his head, it almost seems like the thirteen words are spinning *him*, popping and fizzing in his cranium, disconnecting and reconnecting synapses, introducing neurons to new neighbors.

Connor retires early with a headache. And his dreams are strange.

In the morning, Connor sits at the breakfast table across from his father, munching off-brand corn flakes and marshalling his arguments. Dad, he says, I think we should talk again about sending me to a summer debate institute. And he braces for what will follow. There is no money, of course. There is never money. Since that day, ten years ago, when Connor sat in his first suit at his mother's funeral, Connor's father has worked two and sometimes three jobs to keep food on the table and a roof over their heads. She was the smart one, Connor's father always says, the up-and-coming lawyer. She's the one you take after, son, he says, beaming with pride. Connor's father works with his hands, wearing himself down to a nub in exchange for a fraction of the income she could have earned.

Connor knows, entering into the debate with his father, that he has no chance at a clean win. So he prepares to fight dirty. Connor is prepared to say: Dad, I need to earn a debate scholarship, we can't pay for college any other way. Dad, I know you don't want your grandson to grow up the way I grew up. Dad, this is what mom would have wanted.

Connor braces himself to say these things. Then his father, hard-handed and bleary-eyed from God knows how little sleep, looks up at Connor and says, Yeah, OK. We'll send you to debate camp.

All of Connor's arguments die unuttered. He sits, numb with surprise. Really? He says. Yeah, replies his father. What about the money? Connor asks. His dad sits staring for a moment. Hadn't really thought about it, he says. Which is odd, because Connor knows that his father seldom has the luxury of thinking about anything else.

Connor cracks a joke: Well, in that case, can I have a Maserati, too? His father sits staring for a moment, then nods, stone-faced. Connor waits for him to crack up in laughter, but his father just keeps mechanically shoveling

28

the cereal in. Dad, seriously, Connor says. His father looks up, shrugs. Just makes sense, he replies. A kid's gotta get around somehow, right? Not even a hint of a grin.

Connor tents his fingers in front of his chin, watching as his father slowly, methodically works his way towards the bottom of the bowl. Dad, he says, you should wear that cereal bowl as a hat.

His father looks up, mild surprise in his eyes. Hadn't really thought of it that way, he says. And then his father, who to the best of Connor's recollection hasn't done a single silly thing in the decade since a drunk driver wiped out the love of his life, calmly picks up the bowl in front of him and upends it over his own head. Soggy corn flakes patter against the cheap nylon carpet. Connor's father peers out at him through cascading rivulets of milk, brown eyes solemn, perfectly matter-of-fact. Connor stares back, waiting for a laugh that never comes.

CROSS-EXAMINATION

"The third disadvantage is ecocide. Subpoint A is the nuclear war they prevent. Subpoint B is global climate change. Subpoint C is ozone depletion. Subpoint D is pesticide runoff and oceanic dead zones. Subpoint E is the Pacific trash vortex. Subpoint F is oil spills. Subpoint G is hydraulic fracturing. Subpoint H is deforestation.

Must I go on? Must I exhaust the alphabet as we have exhausted the Earth? The problem, judges, is not that humanity is incapable of love, but that our love is self-directed. Our priority is proximity—family over nation, nation over humanity, humanity over all else that lives. We are incapable of the sort of self-sacrificing love that makes coexistence possible. Nuclear war, I will grant, is not the most environmentally benign of actions, but at least it has the merit of eliminating the cause of all the other problems. Solve the problem, judges, and negate."

Connor and Amit run amok. Their victory of the previous week was hard-won, the result of years of painstaking effort and thirty hours a week of research and practice. This is different.

Connor and Amit's strategy has not evolved. The element of surprise is gone. They have made themselves a stationary target for their opponents' research, and it seems to Connor that their opponents have done an excellent job of preparing, that the responses he and Amit facing are well-reasoned and well-evidenced, that he and Amit are barely winning the argument at the best of times and losing it badly most of the time. The judges, however, disagree. Connor scarcely has time to open his mouth before the judges sign the ballot in his favor. Even his opponents, who have worked so hard developing what seemed to be sound strategies, slump their shoulders at Connor's responses. For Connor, the victories are without savor. The thirteen words hang before him now, always, as if seared into his retinas. What have his accomplishments to do with him?

Amit is thriving amidst the glowing ruins of civilization. Connor once watched Amit, lost in thought, walk directly into a tree, then excuse himself politely and continue on his way. Amit is in love with the abstraction of ideas and the complexity of systems—he will, without provocation, speak at length about the mechanics of a bumblebee's flight or about Bentham's notion of the Panopticon. Now, Amit has fallen in love with the concept of human extinction. It seems to Connor that Amit, who once trailed in his wake, a mere machine to execute Connor's strategies, is beginning to surpass him in skill. It fills Connor with pride to see Amit achieve this, and it saddens him that the judges can't seem to recognize it, that their ballots consistently rank Connor as the superior competitor. But from a win-loss perspective, it makes no difference. Connor and Amit hold their own on the affirmative and wipe everyone out on the negative, winning their second tournament in a row. And after the awards ceremony, Connor goes for the BIG win: he asks Ambriel out to dinner. She accepts, of course, and Connor wishes like hell that the delight in her eyes were the product of his own merit, rather than of a formula someone recited in his ear.

The night arrives; he dresses in his least-wretched outfit, and pilots his shameful jalopy to her family's McMansion, where she waits, resplendent, a golden-skinned figurine, a trophy to be won. Her parents raise an eyebrow at their daughter's scarecrow of a suitor, but he assures them that he's not as bad as appearances would indicate. And they agree; of course they do.

Connor's expectations for Ambriel are unimaginably high. She exceeds them. She is, as far as Connor can tell, perfect in every way. She treats his rusted-out Olds as if it were a coach-and-four, names it "Clarence," and every time they pass through a yellow light, she kisses her palm and presses it to the vehicle's ceiling, leaving Connor jealous of his own dome light. At dinner, she talks easily and freely of matters large and small—so much so that Connor finds himself, entirely against his nature, relaxing. And when the subject matter turns to the weird, wonderful members of the community that they share— Amit, Cece Eberhardy, the Wu brothers, Thoroughly Postmodern Millie Roberts, all the glorious freaks that make up high school debate—the two of them laugh until their sides hurt.

And when, on the ride home, Ambriel turns to Connor with a lopsided grin and asks him to park the car for a while, Connor is so excited that he scarcely notices that what's happening is happening at *her* instigation, not his. She proves confident in all the ways that he is shy, and skillful in all the ways that he is clumsy, and patient with him in all the ways that he is impatient with himself, and when the two of them come up for air for a moment, she tells him that she's been waiting for over a year for him to ask her out. She tells him that he is so, so sexy when he's up there at the podium, interrogating ideas instead of his own flaws. And, miracle of miracles, he actually finds himself *believing* it. And then, somewhat later, Ambriel hands Connor a small foil package, and as he grasps for it with fumbling fingers, he feels the jaws of the trap close around him.

Connor's newfound talent means that Ambriel cannot give him her consent.

31

Or, rather, she cannot *deny* him her consent, or withdraw it. Which is, Connor knows, the same thing. His fantasy is a reality, but he cannot allow himself to live it, because whatever his flaws, his father did not raise him to be a monster.

He pulls away. What's wrong? she asks. Too fast? she asks. Did I blow it? Did I ruin it? Did I mess everything up again? Her perfect composure has evaporated, her face is suddenly and strangely desperate, and he wants, more than anything else, to reassure her.

Except, he thinks. If he does so, she will accept his explanation completely. She will believe any lie or any truth he offers. She will have no power to resist. He loves her face, he loves her body, but above all else, he loves her agency, her fearlessness, her strength of will. And he cannot speak a single sentence to her without destroying all of those things. The two of them will never have a disagreement, never have to hash out a compromise. He will always have his way—and in having it, her will will cease to exist except as an extension of his own. In time, his personality will eclipse hers. His mind will subsume hers. There will cease to be the two of them, and there will instead be two of him.

And he loves her. And he will not make that exchange.

So Connor swallows, and he says, it's not you, it's me. A pathetic cliché, but she believes it.

And Connor says, you have done nothing wrong, and she believes this, too.

And Connor pauses for a long moment, and then he makes himself do it. He says: you deserve better than me. And in saying it, he changes her mind. Her eyes are suddenly wary, and she covers herself up, and she says, take me home. Which he does, in perfect silence; he has already said more than he wished to.

FIRST REBUTTAL

"If the scientists are insufficient to convince you, judges, then, perhaps you'd care to hear from the philosophers? Consider the following critique. We will call it Negative Utilitarianism.

Subpoint A presents a philosophical truth: our primary moral obligation is to minimize suffering. Note that I do NOT say 'to maximize happiness'; the two are not the same. As Hampe and Contestabile demonstrated in 2010, the alleviation of suffering always has a superior moral claim over the provision of pleasure. Consider a starving man seeking a crust of bread, and a healthy man seeking a gourmet meal: are their claims equivalent? Consider a woman dying of cancer and a man with no medical issues; which matters more, her right to relief from pain, or his right to an orgasm?

Subpoint B. Life is pain. Schopenhauer explained: pain insists upon itself, makes itself impossible to ignore; pleasure is defined only by the absence of want or need. All life endures by consuming other life; do you suppose the pleasure experienced by the animal eating is commensurate to the pain of the animal being eaten? Pain, not pleasure, is king.

Subpoint C offers you an alternative to the agony that is life. Instead of the affirmative's policy proposal, which seeks to keep the wheel of suffering spinning, grinding us and our descendants down for all eternity, you can opt for voluntary human extinction, the brainchild of environmentalist Les Knight. Choose not to breed, and to husband Earth's resources as carefully as possible while we remain. What greater gift can we give the generations yet unborn than the absence of their own births, than freedom from their own pain?

You can choose to end suffering, rather than to perpetuate it. You can choose to negate."

In terms of competitive success, Connor and Amit are on a rocket to the moon. Spaceflight, however, has its drawbacks. In the absence of gravity, muscles atrophy. Robbed of the resistance caused by the prospect of a loss, Connor is getting sloppy. He is throwing stuff at the wall, and of course, it is all sticking.

Employing their wipeout strategy, Connor and Amit win their third straight tournament. Amit has never been better. Connor has never been worse. It seems to Connor that their opponents' responses are now very, very good indeed, but of course it has long since ceased to matter how hard their opponents work or what they say. Afterwards, holding the trophy, he is surrounded by admirers and immersed in self-loathing.

At eight PM that evening, the phone rings in Connor's trailer. His father picks up, listens for a moment, then stares, white-faced, at Connor. He hands him the receiver. Connor listens for a moment, then rushes out into the night.

Connor is in the driver's seat of the car he now calls Clarence, its headlights eating up the road before him, and he is remembering another night in the same car, he behind the wheel and Amit in the passenger seat, hopelessly lost on a back road in the hills outside Emporia. If we drive forever, Connor assures Amit, we'll eventually find something. Amit corrects him: if we drive forever, eventually we'll find *everything*.

Connor is thinking of last year's debate team T-shirt, which Amit designed. The front bears a child's scrawl; mixed capitals and lower-case letters, a lopsided smiley face, and the slogan "We liek D3bate alot." The back bears the names of each member of the squad in the same shaky childish hand. Childlike wonder alongside formidable intellect; the capacity both to pick ideas to pieces and to believe in them utterly; the irony of Amit.

Connor is thinking of his father. Once so strong, a lifetime of work in hazardous environments, with heavy objects, with toxic chemicals, have taken their toll. And when his father thinks he's not looking, Connor sees the signs: the tremors in his once steady hand, the subtle twitching on the left side of his face. Connor thinks of the movie he once saw in which the pirate built up an immunity to small doses of poison over the years, and knows it for a lie. A tiny dose of death might be endured. But the doses do not dissipate with time. They accumulate, a snowball rolling downhill. They build momentum. They overwhelm.

And Connor is remembering an event from his early childhood, before the loss of his mother: he and Amit, side by side on a riverbank, high above the water, wearing swimming trunks. A rope dangling from a tree limb in

34

front of them; if they dare swing from it, it will project them out into empty space. Connor knock-kneed, afraid; Amit, half his size, reassuring him. *Don't be afraid, Connor. I'll go first.*

When Connor arrives at the hospital and rushes through the emergency room door, a huge throng rises to greet him. His teammates, yes, but also all of the others, all the competitors from neighboring schools, all of the people Connor and Amit have been wiping out on a weekly basis. The nerd-horde. The Wus are there, of course, and Bobby Throckmorton, Amanda and Maggie and LaToya and Tony, and yes, even Ambriel, over there in the corner, her eyes red. All of them, dozens upon dozens, all of his allies and all of his enemies, along with a horde of JV kids and pimply-faced freshmen he's never even met. He scarcely recognizes them without their three-piece suits and prim, pleated skirts, without the laptop glow lighting up their faces. It's Ambriel, of course, who has the courage to meet his wild-eyed, desperate gaze, and who swallows slowly, and shakes her head before she dissolves back into tears, taking half the room with her. But, of course, she need not have bothered. Connor knew, from the moment he heard the tremulous voice on the phone, how it would end. Because Amit was always impeccably careful, precise in everything he did; he would have researched the process carefully and known exactly how to wield the razor blade, exactly how to put the process beyond the possibility of chance or retrieval. Amit was firmly resolved.

There is no strength in Connor's legs, but he manages to make his way across the room to the bench on which Amit's parents huddle, arms around each other, in a paroxysm of grief. And he sits down silently beside them and waits to be noticed, and when he is, they instantly open up to enfold him as well, their son's best friend and idol, Amit's link to a community in which his intellect was nourished and his nature understood. And when, at length, they can bear to release him, Amit's father reaches into his pocket and withdraws a crumpled piece of paper torn from a yellow legal pad, and hands it with fumbling fingers to Connor, and stares at him, his eyes desperate for understanding. And Connor looks down at the paper, and the words on it, written in a calm, decisive hand, read: I am completely convinced.

And Connor is up and out the door, the pleas of his friends fading behind him, drowned out by the roar of his car's engine as he streaks across town, heedless of traffic, to fulfill a promise he made a decade ago, a promise he made as a seven-year-old boy sitting at a funeral wearing his first suit. He has always had the motive, now he has the mechanism, and there is certainly no reason not to act. It is, in the debater's parlance, try or die.

SECOND REBUTTAL

"The fourth disadvantage, judges, is Antimatter Cascade. Here, again, we offer you three lines of analysis. Subpoint A: the affirmative plan prevents a nuclear war. Subpoint B: In the absence of nuclear war, antimatter weapons will be developed. Lin Xe demonstrated in 2014 that, on our current trajectory, we are mere years away from the ability to harness matter-antimatter explosions. And, Subpoint C: A war with antimatter weapons produces limitless destruction. As Professor Delgado of the University of California at Bakersfield shows, the potential energy of a matter-antimatter detonation is ten billion times that of an equivalent quantity of high explosive, and an explosion involving antimatter poses a threat to the baryonic matter of which the universe is composed.

It is a fundamental constant of human experience: if a thing exists, we will weaponize it. Humanity will miss no opportunity to turn its abilities to destructive purposes. The time has come to end that destruction by ending ourselves. You must negate."

The trailer park is not so different from the one in which Connor resides. This particular unit is more dilapidated than most, the patchy grass around it cluttered with windblown trash and aluminum cans. When Connor hammers on the door, it nearly comes off its decaying hinges. The man who opens it has gone to fat;

he is unshaven in a sleeveless T-shirt, his hair a greying, cottony fringe, a rich man's caricature of poverty, and his right shoulder bears a crude tattoo of the sort one gets in prison. The face has changed, but not so greatly that Connor does not recognize it, from that courtroom in which he and his father sat, side by side, ten years ago.

This man had no words for Connor and his father that day, merely an apology mumbled off of an index card before they shuffled him off to a pitifully short term behind bars. He has long since emerged from prison, free to live the life that his neglect denied to Connor's mother. And there has been no sign, no sign whatsoever, that he will make anything of that life. His license has been suspended, and restored, and suspended again; he has been back in jail and out again, and he has been in but mostly out of work, and in but mostly out of rehab. Connor knows this, because Connor has been watching this man, quite meticulously, for ten years, waiting for his opportunity. And here it is.

And Connor opens his mouth to speak. At what he means to say is: you should kill yourself.

And the words won't come.

A lifetime spent husbanding his rage. Years spent arming himself with words, sharpening his vocabulary like a prison shank. A childhood spent learning to set his feelings aside in order to win the argument; to appear placid on the surface while churning underneath, to say what needs to be said. All that time, polishing his skills to be able to cut creatures like this one down to size, developing the gifts that are his only legacy from his mother. And now, at the critical moment, with nothing left to lose and no other future to anticipate, the words won't come. He is his mother's son, but his father's as well, and the last words Connor ever intends to speak won't come.

And what comes dribbling out of his mouth instead is: you should stop drinking.

Connor turns tail and flees, leaving behind him a worn and confused figure who will never consume another drop of alcohol. And Connor and Clarence are on the road again, and when he finally gets back to his own trailer, his father is gone, of course; Connor's desperate friends have called his home and his father is out searching for him. And Connor cannot find any razor blades in the bathroom, but his father has been working construction and has left a linoleum knife on the carpet not far from the door. Connor spots the knife and picks it up. He looks around at the interior of the trailer. His father always keeps it immaculate. So Connor heads outside instead.

He has one final article to cut.

THIRD REBUTTAL

"The fifth and final disadvantage, judges, is Invasive Species.

Subpoint A is the nuclear war. The affirmative preserves the human race.

Subpoint B is the aliens. The Sagan evidence indicates that in a universe of this size, the emergence of life on thousands of worlds is a virtual certainty. Many civilizations must have already arisen that match or exceed ours in technological capacity. Yet we have not discovered any. Scientists call it the Fermi paradox: if aliens are possible, then where are they? Advanced civilizations cannot conceivably be unaware of humanity; we have been beaming electromagnetic evidence of our existence into the beyond for many decades. We have sought them aggressively. Why do they not answer? It can only be because they are in hiding. They have decoded our radio transmissions, our television broadcasts, our cultural representations of ourselves, and they recognize us for what we are: a threat to all that lives.

Subpoint C: Humanity is an invasive species. We are, at present, only capable of wrecking one planet, but nothing lasts forever. We are the disease against which the universe has no antibodies. Should we survive to the point of achieving interstellar travel, we will reenact the conquest of the Americas on a galactic scale. It will be the greatest atrocity in the history of the universe. You must amputate the gangrenous limb that is humanity to protect the greater body of lifekind.

38

You must negate. If you won't defend the aliens against us, who will?"

Darkness, and the bitter taste of antiseptic, and the sterile bleeping of machines.

Connor awakes to white light and shadowy figures surrounding his bedside. His mouth feels as if it is stuffed with cotton. After a few woozy moments, he discovers the source of this feeling: his mouth *is*, in fact, stuffed with cotton, thick rolls of gauze to bind up his self-inflicted wound.

A nurse, her eyes a strange shade of hazel, almost gold, announces to a nearby doctor that the patient is awake. She steps away from Connor's bedside, then out of the room. Connor, hazy with painkillers, hears the doctor address his father. He hears that he is fortunate, all things considered; he passed out from pain and shock well before he was able to saw entirely through the muscle. There will be long, difficult months of rehab ahead. Connor's career as a debater is certainly over, but with painstaking work, he may one day be able to speak almost normally.

His father stares down at him, eyes glassy. Features haggard. He has been without sleep for some unguessable length of time. Son, he says, why? Why would you hurt yourself? Didn't I tell you I would pay for the camp? Didn't I tell you I would buy the Maserati?

Slowly, through the haze, as if to apologize, Connor raises his hand to take his father's. His own hand is soft, has never known greater trauma than the touch of a keypad; his father's is a mass of callus and scar tissue, the fingers crooked from work-related fractures and dislocations. Connor sucks in air through his nose and, through the cotton, emits three strangled, guttural grunts.

The words don't come, but Connor's father understands them anyway. And when he does, he closes his eyes wearily, raises his free hand to idly massage his own left temple. No, son, he says. I don't believe you. No, you do not love me. Because you remember what it was like without her. And if you loved me, you would never deprive me of you, the way we were deprived of her.

39

And Connor begins to cry. He cries because of the pain he has caused, and because of the pain he has suffered. He cries because he knows that the persuasive task ahead of him is the most important he will ever confront. His case will be a difficult one, and he will have to be both his own advocate and the author of his own evidence.

But Connor also cries with joy. Because someone, finally, has learned to say no to him. And it seems to Connor that he has never heard a more beautiful sound than that of the word No.

FINAL FOCUS

"Williamson in '92: 'Our deepest fear is not that we are inadequate. Our deepest fear is that we are powerful beyond measure.'

You must negate."

The nurse proceeds to a nearby corridor, then to a service elevator, in the corner of which sits a black duffel bag. She enters alone, and the doors close behind her. As it descends to the basement, her facial features shift subtly, then blur. She reaches for the duffel bag with six-fingered hands, regards it through shining golden eyes, and withdraws a janitor's coverall. She lifts her nurse's cap from the scaly indigo crest that ridges her head and casts it aside. She recalls whispering in the boy's unconscious ear, inflicting seven words on his subconscious mind, earlier that afternoon.

The plan was sound. Her superiors will understand. Humanity's leaders achieve their status by mouthing vapid platitudes. Truly revolutionary thought, truly *dangerous* thought, is the province of the young, and the power to choose tomorrow's leaders is the power to own the future. But the boy, she reflects, was a disappointment. He might have been the one. His thought process had shown special potential. But in the end, it had been necessary to turn him off; he showed signs of turning the gift towards unproductive ends. Still,

40

she thinks, there will be others. In the end, humanity's attraction to apocalypse is insatiable.

The affirmative will have its day. But the negative only has to win once.

Ecotastrophe II
Edited by J Alan Erwine

The planet seems in even greater peril, and maybe we are facing Ecotastrophe, but is there time to save ourselves.

Ecotastrophe II features startling fiction from Tyree Campbell, Dan Rice, Melanie Rees, Robert J. Mendenhall, Gustavo Bondoni, and Mike Adamson.

Order a copy here today:
   https://www.hiraethsffh.com/product-
   page/ecotastrophe-2-edited-by-j-alan-erwine

Occupant of the Red Chamber

Scott J. Couturier

A weeping ghost in a remote red room
manifests with no eye to see.
Sorrowful she drifts athwart centuried gloom,
enduring an austere eternity.

Only thrice has she ever been beheld
by mortal gaze – imbuing fright!
Yet, an untold number of nights she's wailed,
oft audible after out-blown light.

Dim drapes of cobweb are long-settled there,
where no stray sunbeam cares to fall,
a decades-sealed chamber renowned as where
horrid things happened: blood-stained walls.

Yet – forever must she mourn. *How* she mourns
in seclusion total, amid decaying silks,
soul deformed beyond Death's easeful bourne
to a bitterness sere as serpent's milk.

The Language of Machines
Lawrence Buentello

The Crash

The crew came awake as the claxon beat the first warning: the ship was failing.

Helena's stasis bed reformed into her command chair as she struggled to clear her perceptions—the metronomic pulse of the claxon beat again through her head, as if she were inside a giant drum. Once the chair slid into position beside the sensor array, she activated her interface with the ship's controls as the other members of the crew achieved their positions in the cabin. No one had time to say a word, let alone acknowledge the possibility of potential disaster—the four men and four women routinely began their internal assessment of the instrumentation as their training required. Each was assigned an aspect of the ship and its corpus—navigation, propulsion, life support systems, mechanical integrity—and each, in turn, was trained to address any issues that might arise.

From her chair, Helena inspected the oncoming star system the ship's artificial brain had guided them toward after dropping out of zero-point space. The ship had assessed the potential of each body in the system and determined that the planetary body to which they were moving best met the requirements for an emergency landing. The planet, 1.3 times the mass of the Earth, possessed a suitable atmosphere, though anomalies in the chemical spectrum puzzled her. She didn't have time to assess these anomalies, though, before Timus announced to each crew member simultaneously: *The core is melting down.*

Further assessments of the atmosphere were almost certainly superfluous.

Aatha reported: *I'm maintaining navigation toward the ship's selected body. Timus, engage primary engine shut down as soon as we've achieved atmospheric entry. We'll attempt to land without primary.*

Helena sat back in her chair and exhaled heavily. She realized that they were all going to die. The probability of successfully landing a ship with a failing core on an unknown world was phenomenally poor. In fact, she knew of no ship that had survived a core meltdown. The crew was following protocol, as it was trained to, but each crew member surely realized the inevitability of their deaths.

She had a difficult time countering the anxiety that swept through her body, but managed to retain her composure. It was important to her to die well-composed and performing her duties until the very last moment. She followed the sensor readings until the planet expanded in her perceptions, which were, after all, the sensory perceptions of the ship's instruments. She felt an irresistible urge to cry out to the other crew members, a word of goodbye, or to tell them how gratified she was to have served with them on their mission. But she calmed herself and remained silent.

As the ship slipped into the planet's atmosphere, the claxon still bleating its warning of impending death, she sensed something strange from the planet's terrain—an impossible uniformity not belonging to ordinary geological land masses or churning bodies of liquid. The surface of the planet toward which their ship hurtled was suffused by perfect geometrical shapes—but that was impossible—

Aatha said: *Prepare for landing. Assume impact positions. Enact emergency escape procedures once the ship has landed.*

Helena's chair enveloped her in its emergency restraints, pushing her down into the contoured material and sliding the impact form over her body. The impact of atmospheric gases against the ship's hull overpowered her senses; her last coherent thoughts were of the faces of her shipmates, and of how much she would miss them, before the secondary landing jets failed to mitigate the ship's impact with the surface of the world.

When the ship fragmented, she fell into a thoughtless, senseless void.

She couldn't know that these would represent her last moments fixed in a familiar human reality.

Awakening

Helena fought to understand her sensual perceptions, mostly failing, but at times registering a piece of information that eventually joined with those already collected to present a quasi-impression of the world. First, her eyes saw only a hazy white light, which may have been the ceiling of a room, or the overcast cloud-cover of an unfocused sky; after a while she realized she was lying supine, though she couldn't immediately feel her limbs. Then a soft buzzing tickled her ears, a steady, mechanical sound like the droning of bees; and, finally, an odd scent joined her inhalations, reminding her of the sterile smell of a laboratory or medical facility.

She couldn't move, in fact, she felt paralyzed, but not panicked. She simply felt no anxiety, which shouldn't have been the case, especially after having crash-landed on an alien world. She sensed that she was still breathing, but the generalized white expanse filling her field of vision offered no indication of her physical disposition.

How long she lay in this position she didn't know. She felt herself slipping in and out of consciousness regularly, and had no notion as to the duration of the passing time. She did, however, have a sense that *something* was moving around her, though it remained invisible even in her peripheral vision, a shadow accompanying the odd buzzing noise, the sound intensifying as she felt the presence moving near her, and then subsiding as she felt the presence moving away.

She realized, too, after a time, that her thought processes were not functioning normally—she had no capacity for analytical thought, and when she tried to sort the memories shifting through her conscious mind she could barely hold the image of a face, or a name, or any part of her personal history that might help explain her circumstances.

Was she dead?

No, she still sensed her own respiration, so she couldn't be—

And then, after waking from one of her sleeping states,

her memory returned—she remembered awakening aboard ship with the claxon beating and her shipmates struggling to regain control of their doomed craft—she remembered everything now—

And gasped, and drew in a great gulp of air, and pushed herself up on her elbows. The hazy white expanse vanished, replaced by a shimmering pale blue sky above, and all around her, as she turned her head from side to side, massive structures, cylindrical towers, domed structures and gigantic cubes and looming pyramids, all clad in a soft, shimmering white material as delicate and intricate as mother-of-pearl.

Amazed, she leaned forward and struggled to her knees. Then the pain hit, and she doubled over, her face hanging near the ground, which, too, was composed of the same glimmering white material. She wrapped her arms around her torso, gasping again, remembering the crash and her expectation of coming death. And though the pain was pervasive, throbbing in her joints, along her bones, burning over her skin, she found no visible injuries when she finally examined her hands, arms, when she drew her fingertips over her face—she found only one change on her body when she pulled her hands over the top of her head: her hair, which she'd kept short enough to accommodate onboard regulations, was gone, as if she'd been finely shaved. She realized, too, that she was dressed in the same environmental suit and footwear she'd worn aboard ship, though when she examined the deep red material closely she discovered innumerable rends had been repaired, as if the tears were melted together by some force.

When she accepted the pain as a more or less permanent condition, she decided she may as well obey her training despite her discomfort. She stood, testing the integrity of her legs, and finally turned a full circle, studying the world around her.

She was breathing the alien atmosphere, though her sensor readings while aboard ship indicated that should have been impossible, and she was most definitely alive. She didn't believe in an afterlife for human beings, or any beings for that matter, and felt certain she was standing in a real, physical environment. But this environment made little sense. If this was a city, it was not a city for beings with human dimensions—the huge structures, which she compared with the typical buildings of a Terran city, held no doors or windows. Seamless, they seemed as if they were constructed from solid material, though it was a material with which she wasn't familiar.

And the structures, which dwarfed her, were not laid out in the typical grid arrangement of a true city. Instead, they all occupied their own irregular space upon the endless plain of white material, some structures having a large amount of space separating their foundations, and some buttressed against one another. There seemed no sense in the distribution of these buildings, if they were indeed buildings, but alien geometries did not necessarily have to obey human logistics.

She turned, and turned, and turned again, but simply couldn't understand what had happened to her, or where she was—and then she thought: *where is the rest of my crew?*

Sudden fear subdued the ache in her bones and lay unmoving in her stomach.

Helena was alone.

Exploration

Her isolation was not of first importance. Around her, a geometric maze rose and fell like hills and valleys composed only of straight lines. She walked between the 'buildings' seeking a portal or window, any access that might avail her of the inhabitants of this city. But there were no doors or windows. Each featureless plain of *material*—after touching the buildings, she could no longer call the substance of which the shapes were composed *metal*—bore no features, and because it didn't seem to reflect electromagnetic radiation aside from muted visible light, she decided the material must be designed to absorb significant solar energy. For what reason, she didn't know, since none of it seemed to have an outlet.

I'm a rat in a maze.

But she knew this feeling was only the convenient

hypothesis of a desperate mind. If she were indeed alive, she was the survivor of a crash landing on the surface of an alien world. But if that were true, where was the rest of her crew or the substantial remains of their interstellar ship? No, she did not believe in an afterlife. If she had died in the landing she would have no perceptions. And the terrible ache she felt in her body was proof enough of life.

Wherever she walked she found the same unrelenting plain of pearlescent structures, massive cubes, smaller orbs, rising towers that seemed to have no purpose other than to stand as silhouettes in the subdued natural light. She periodically called out, painfully, because her throat exhibited the same ache as the rest of her body, asking if anyone could hear her, see her, acknowledge her, but received no reply. She walked for hours, hoping to find some variance in the structures, but found no differentiation whatsoever; not even her footsteps echoed between the high walls. The only sound she heard was her own rasping exhalations as she continued her exploration.

When she grew tired, she stopped and sat on the ground. She rubbed her face and performed mental exercises designed to stay panic, exercises she'd been trained to perform when confronted by difficult environmental dilemmas. Once she'd calmed herself, she gazed up at the hazy sky and realized she was thirsty. Then she understood the simple mathematical fact: she was a biological entity in a world without biology. And since the structures, though beautiful, were as useful to an organic life form as a sterile desert, she would soon perish from thirst or hunger.

My survival will be a short-term proposition. Maybe that's for the best.

Then, in a measure that may have been desperation, she called out, "Someone help me! I need water! I need water to drink, or I'll die!"

She envisioned the water dispenser from her ship— she'd always thought the recycled water was too metallic tasting, too antiseptic, but now she longed for it, for only a drink. But as the memory of the ship's water rose in her mind, she also felt a strange sensation in her head, as if the neural interface implanted in her brain, with which she communicated with the ship's computers, had suddenly flared to life.

Even as she was studying this new physical sensation, something finally changed in her environment. She felt a subtle vibration beneath her, as if the ground were gently shifting. She placed the flat of her palms against the material, trying to sense the intention of the movement, but then the vibration subsided and the world once again petrified. She was too surprised to do much more than sit and wait—someone, or something seemed to have responded to her outcry. Helena had communicated in some way with the inhabitants of this world, which gave her an uprising of hope that adequately muted her physical pain.

When the ground unexpectedly morphed before her feet, she tried to crawl away from the effect. But the effect wasn't threatening—before her a concave indentation formed in the ground, as if miraculously sunken from below. She observed this phenomenon cautiously, rising to her knees and preparing to defend herself if necessary. But as she watched, the indentation, which she now understood to be a bowl formed from the very substance of the ground, began filling with clear liquid. Once the liquid filled to the level of the surrounding terrain it ceased and stood glimmering in the weak starlight.

Amazed, she crept forward on her hands and knees, wary of surprises, but then she lowered her face to the liquid and inhaled. The faint scent of ozone rose from the bowl, the familiar smell of recycled water. Incapable of understanding how this manifestation was possible, she dipped a finger into the liquid and dabbed her fingertip against the tip of her tongue. Aside from a slightly metallic taste, one very similar to the taste of the water produced by the ship's onboard processors, she decided it was indeed water, and bent low enough to drink down a mouthful. *Water.* She had asked for water, and water had appeared before her. Why? Had someone read her thoughts? No, telepathy was only a fictional method of communication.

She hadn't realized she was so thirsty. She drank her fill, wondering if any more water would appear later. When she was done, she sat back on the ground and watched as the water remaining in the bowl slowly reabsorbed into the material from which it came and the indentation subsided as if inflated from below.

Her spoken request for water should have been ignored. No one could have known her true need who didn't understand her language. So how had her invocation been understood? Had the world's inhabitants comprehended the potential of her implanted neural interface and sensed her biological needs?

Despite this mystery, Helena realized she'd just communicated practically with whomever monitored the city. Surely, then, she could communicate in other ways. She would come to understand where she was in the galaxy, the location of her crew, and, if possible, she might even be able to discover a way to initiate her rescue.

Communications

She continued walking through the 'city', which was nothing more than a perpetual landscape of the strangely constructed structures, her vision saved from the sameness of her environment by the varying geometry. If the structures had been too uniform she might have begun hallucinating as one does in an endless sweep of desert sands or a continuous plain of arctic ice. There seemed no end to the vistas of structures, and several times she simply stopped and sat pondering the immensity of the world in which she found herself.

She had lost any concept of having moved away from the place where she'd regained consciousness. That point seemed identical to this point, or any other point she might achieve in her travels.

When she thirsted, she envisioned the water in her lost ship, and a new pool of water formed before her.

And after many hours, when she hungered, she envisioned the small food stores in the ship, sweet and savory nutrition bars that were the crew's main source of sustenance when not held in physical suspension, and as if by magic a small square of some substance seemed to issue from the ground.

The first time one of these food squares appeared, she examined it carefully, noting the lack of odor and the dissimilarity of texture. Again, the neural interface seemed to come to life within her skull when she envisioned the food, and again a tangible version of her thoughts had manifested. After calculating the possibility of holding a poisonous creation in her hands, she decided that because the water had been consumable this new facsimile might also be innocuous. She broke off a piece of the bar and slowly chewed it, not entirely pleased by the taste, but not repelled enough to spit it out. She swallowed, and then, hoping she was making the right decision, she ate the rest.

And then ate another bar when she grew hungry again, and another, without ill effect.

These experiments showed Helena that her 'monitors' were, in some way, concerned for her well-being, and meant her no harm. At any time they could have silenced her, or watched her die of thirst. She wondered why she didn't feel a variance of temperature or air quality, since the sky seemed opened to her, but long observation of the sky above the city provided a variety of light tones that could only be differentiated through careful study. She finally concluded that during the nocturnal hours the material of the buildings emanated a variable luminescence that closely matched the rising and setting of the planet's star, so that at no time did the surface of the city, and perhaps even the world, find itself in darkness.

Despite the lack of night, she still slept when her body grew weary. On waking, she began to believe that the cityscape had subtly changed around her, and she verified this by carefully memorizing the positions of the towers to her north and south and finding them decidedly shifted along the axis of her stationary body.

She didn't understand why the structures should spontaneously shift, nor the spectacular mechanics behind such a set of circumstances. For such immense structures to shift at will seemed impossible.

Helena thought of her crew often, and wondered, as she walked, if she would ever see them again, or if they had survived the landing. She used her scientific training to the best of her ability, but even with profound skills and high intelligence, her emotional state began deteriorating and she found herself depressed and increasingly hopeless. No other beings seemed to wish to engage her, no matter how often she spoke into the air. No form of communication she tried seemed to bring a practical response.

Once, in a loss of self-control, she found herself crying out, "Can anyone hear me! Can anyone understand me! Please, show yourselves! Please, come talk to me! Help me!"

She turned in a circle, her hands cupped to her mouth, shouting her needs over and over again, but received no response.

After awhile, emotionally exhausted, she sat on the ground like a frightened child and cried. She thought of Timus, Aatha, Odin, Hesti, Gaspara, Inkira, and Patrice, and wept for their company.

When her emotional breakdown concluded, and she found herself again in the same place where she'd begun, surrounded by iridescent towers, buildings, and domes of magnificent architecture, she calmly assessed her situation and knew she was due to fulfill her role as planetary explorer, even if only in her mind. After all, she had nothing but time to consider her surroundings.

Helena concluded the following: That if this world were governed by hidden intelligences, they had decided not to expose themselves to her, or communicate in any complex way. That the status of the technology before her clearly delineated a superior civilization capable of manufacturing highly advanced scientific invention, far beyond that of Earth. And that because she had food to eat, water to drink, and air to breathe, this civilization seemed to want to see to her needs, despite not wanting to contact her directly.

Perhaps she was only a specimen to them; but that seemed unlikely. If she were, they wouldn't have a need for her to remain living, or if they wished to study her, why not do so in confinement? Why let her roam at will within their world?

Or perhaps she was simply sensing this world through a virtual simulation and lay unconscious in some laboratory. She wished for this last possibility to be true, since that meant she might eventually arise from such a state, though it was highly improbable.

Of course, Helena lost track of time.

Without a discernible day and night in the city, with no chronograph, and no way to use the appearance of the native star to measure the passing of time, she could only guess at the length of her stay on the world. So she invented, in her mind, a series of experiments to test the impassivity of her observers.

She sat cross-legged on the ground meditatively, though concentrating on sending static images through her neural network (assuming all the while that it had been accessed in some way by those watching her). First, she envisioned two human beings communicating through an electronic medium: then she envisioned numeric values in the form of ones and zeroes repeating binary sequences. 00110001 00101011 00110001 00111101 00110010. She mentally repeated this simple formulation religiously until joining the previous image with it. Perhaps, if those receiving her communication understood her intent, she might encourage them to communicate with her directly.

But her efforts at initiating one-on-one communication proved fruitless. No beings appeared before her, only food and water.

Exhausted, she slept, but woke to the same unending city.

Finally, Helena came to a terrifying conclusion.

From her cause-and-effect relationship with her surrounding environment, she realized the possibility was extremely high that there *weren't* any organic natives of the planet, that the natives of the planet were standing right in front of her the entire time. The buildings, the towers, the fantastic pearlescent facades *were* the inhabitants of the planet. This was an automated world, fully functional in itself, serving an unknown purpose, perhaps as a way station for intelligent beings. The technology maintained itself in some unknown way, perhaps through an artificial intelligence that kept the structures in repair.

That was likely, wasn't it?

No. She realized, with a slowly growing fear barely suppressed in her subconscious thoughts, that she had been rescued from the ship's crash landing. And if that were true, it would seem logical that a way station would provide for space travelers in distress—but that would also mean that some practical interface would exist so those travelers would be able to call for assistance or provide for their well-being in the worst of circumstances. Nothing of the sort had manifested for her. The machines beneath the guise of the structures had saved her, but that was as far as their intervention had been deemed necessary. They had no interest in 'rescuing' her. Something else was at play.

The technological entity that was the world had managed to interpret her immediate needs—her mechanical needs, as found within an organic structure. Food, air, and water had been provided for her survival. But these materials could easily be allocated to an equation of mechanics, substituting flesh and bone for metal and machinery.

Somehow, the city had saved her from the wreck of her ship, utilizing its own advanced technology, and provided for her—perhaps as it would have for any other part of the city. And what of her shipmates? The wreckage of her ship? Why had she been removed from these things?

Following the logic of her experience, she concluded, her heart heavy in her chest, that she alone was the only thing the city had found worth preserving. Everyone else must be dead.

No, I'm wrong. I must be wrong.

It had to be another way, a way she hadn't calculated. But she couldn't prove a negative, so Helena began to carefully formulate an experiment that might prove her thesis.

Desperation

If she was correct, then the 'city' would respond to her

communications only in a manner in which it was capable of manifesting within itself.

So instead of creating binary messages in her mind, she stood concentrating on manifesting responses to her thoughts of the city.

Helena's first experiment began by her carefully marking the positions of the structures surrounding her; then she envisioned specific structures changing positions or even changing form. Nothing came of her meditations initially, but she persisted, knowing that the 'intelligence' of the city might have difficulty interpreting her request.

She needed all her resolve to remain standing still when she noticed the first building, a small tower, subtly shift within her peripheral vision.

"Yes," she said, encouraged by her success. "Yes, that is what I mean."

Helena continued ordering the imagery in her mind to accelerate the changes of positions of the structures, and soon they were slowly rotating past her field of vision as if the very material from which they were constructed possessed the ability to spontaneously morph. Perhaps not 'at will', but 'when instructed'. Perhaps, too, all the buildings could receive her thoughts and act on their impressions. Soon, the towers, domes, and buildings were flowing past her like magma, never defacing, but nonetheless animate. Their ability to achieve this state was beyond her technical knowledge.

When she ceased concentrating, her head aching with the effort, the movement of the structures slowed, and then stopped altogether.

Time passed: how much, she didn't know. But she managed to produce other effects reinforcing her theory.

She envisioned the 'ground' at her feet forming itself into a chair on which she could sit, and eventually a chair appeared; she envisioned the form of a 'bed' on which she could sleep, and one appeared; any geometrical shape she could envision formed from the material of the planet surrounding her, but after awhile the novelty of this gift waned, and she realized these new shapes were only alternate manifestations of the original city-scape.

One 'day' Helena stood before one of the tallest towers

she'd yet to encounter and, through long hours of concentration, managed to have a small platform extend before her and slowly rise against the face of the tower of which it was part. This glorious ascension thrilled her like a carnival ride, but when she reached the apex of the tower, and could see over the maze of structures, her thrill changed to dejection—all the way to the horizon, as far as she could see, the world was covered by the anonymous structures, endless kilometers of geometrical shapes, no gaps, no variations, no oceans or bodies of water. The entire surface of the world before her was occupied by the same monotonous technology.

She descended in the same manner, though when she stood on the 'ground' again she struggled with conflicted emotions.

She replicated her experiments enough times to satisfy a scientific appreciation for her current reality—and then, because she was an organic entity, a human being, she fell to despair.

No one was coming to rescue her—the crews of ships on interstellar voyages were required to accept the potential of being lost between worlds. The distances were so vast that rescue was a logical impossibility. Only accidents occurring in local space possessed the potential for intervention.

Helena was far from Earth, and alone.

Only memories of her life remained with her to remind her of her humanity, her childhood on Earth, her extensive training into adulthood, the relationships she'd made during her training flights in local space, and finally her assignment to interstellar missions exploring habitable worlds light-years from Sol. Walking on the plains of worlds trillions of kilometers from her home planet, studying wild variations of flora and fauna, fulfilling her dream of being part of a renaissance of exploration throughout the galaxy. And sharing her experiences with her shipmates, her friends and lovers. This was a life, and these were experiences, she would never know again.

Time continued to pass, long, unbearable, empty days

of mere existence, during which she had only herself to talk to. She knew it was only a matter of time before she lost the ability to think and act rationally. Profound isolation, at least, for human beings, was essentially a death sentence. So why live a tortuous existence until she lost her mind?

Resignation

She resigned herself to death.

She neither ate nor drank, but simply lay on the ground staring up at the sky, waiting to die. The 'city' must have recognized her inertness, but certainly wouldn't be able to understand her intent. *A machine can't understand human motivation.*

Helena lay beneath the immutable sky, feeling her body growing weaker, the pain of her unquenched thirst aching in her throat. She slept, and woke, and slept again, until she felt herself sicken with hunger and thirst. Wasting to death was an extremely painful way to expire, but she was determined to cut off her days of endless psychological misery. Drowsing, she prepared to die.

But she didn't die.

Even through her dissociated state of perception, brought on by a lack of water, she sensed the cloud forming above her, a gas-like fog swirling, having emanated from the ground around her. The fog seemed to possess self-animation, again, an impossibility, and slowly, gently, began falling over her, invading her nostrils, her dry, open mouth. Still weak, and dazed, she felt the fog condensing inside her, down her esophagus and within her stomach. After a while, the fog suffused within her, her thirst abated, and she lost consciousness.

When she woke—unaware of the length of her sleep— she sat up, refreshed, neither thirsty nor hungry.

Whether or not the city had surmised her intent, it had certainly calculated the effect of a lack of food and water on her system, and moved to counteract the effect. *I want to die, don't you understand?*

The city would not allow her to refuse to take sustenance.

Does it see me as a part of itself?

Perhaps that was the answer, a simple, logical equation that caused it to react by 'repairing' a damaged piece of machinery. But she wasn't a machine. She was a human being.

If they wouldn't let her die of self-neglect, there was nothing they could do to counteract Newtonian physics.

When her strength returned, she rose once again to the top of a tower on an elevated extension, but her intent was not to survey the world.

Abruptly, having deliberately cleansed her mind of any conscious thoughts, she lurched off the platform at its apex and tumbled into the air.

The physics of her position in open space were, it seemed, instantly calculated, so, too, the result of her collision with the ground. How the machinery beneath the structures could instantaneously understand the implications of her predicament and just as instantly respond was again beyond her understanding, but she didn't fall to her death as she'd intended. Instead, in an instant, a projection from the tower extended beneath her fall, catching her and decelerating in time to prevent her from injuring herself.

Now lying on the ground, amazed that she was still alive, Helena marveled at the technological complexity and capability of the alien world. Then she sat up and began weeping.

Over time she tested the city's reflexes repeatedly, running head-first into one of the buildings in order to crush her own skull, only to have the structure's wall recede from her more quickly than she could move against it. Nor could she find any straight edge against which to open a vein. None of her attempts to physically harm herself proved effective.

The city simply wouldn't allow her to kill herself.

Redemption

Helena sat holding her head in her hands, desperately trying to find some logical approach to her situation. *Will I*

58

have to wait to grow old to die? Surely the machines couldn't keep her alive forever. *Could they?*

This concept, despite the horror inherent in its possibility, brought something else to mind, an intuitive thought, an *inspiration* of the kind perhaps experienced only by organic beings. She lowered her hands and nodded to herself. How had the city *initially* saved her? Her ship must have suffered catastrophic damage, and so, too, its crew. Seven other people were aboard with her— why was she the only one to survive? Had she been the only fortunate crew member?

It analyzed our remains. It must have.

Her remains must have been the most complete of the crew. Logic dictated—at least, the logic of a mechanical intellect—that one whole machine could be created from the available organic 'parts'. She remembered the nearly unbearable pain she'd experienced on first waking in this world—the ache she still felt in her bones—and realized this must be the case. The city must have analyzed every fragment of the destroyed ship, too, and found remnants of food and water, perhaps even preserved information retrieved from the ship's library.

If those remains once existed, they might still exist.

She stood and focused her thoughts, envisioning the same rushing by of structures, but adding the clear image of body parts and the wreckage of the ship being brought to her within one of the buildings. She closed her eyes and concentrated, and would not stop thinking of the faces of her crewmates no matter how much time passed.

Nothing happened for a very long time, and she was almost resigned to failure, when the structures began to suddenly shift around her.

The ground on which she stood seemed to glide forward; she pinioned to balance herself, and finally knelt on one knee to keep from toppling. The ground beneath her moved with increasing speed, the towers and buildings before her parting like water in the wake of a boat, until the ground ceased moving and she stood before a large, rectangular building undistinguished from any of the others.

Abruptly, the face of this building shimmered and a

portal manifested like water melting a cube of sugar.

Reluctantly, she stepped forward through the opening, strangely gladdened by this welcome variation in the city's nightmarish monotony, but fearful of what she might find. Inside the building, she stood in a large recess illuminated by the glow of the interior material. Before her, hung in a complex latticework of crystalline webs, she found the remains of her crew.

What the city might interpret from her heavy weeping she couldn't have cared less—she put her hands to her face and cried before the fragments of mutilated muscle and bone. Pieces of uniform lay folded beneath the remains. The only crewmember she recognized in the collection of body parts was poor Aatha, half her face suspended in the lattice, partially singed. The city had collected the remains, examined them, then preserved them in some material unlike that of the structures.

When Helena composed herself again, she stepped forward to try to touch a mutilated hand levitating before her, but couldn't penetrate the airy substance of the latticework with her fingers. She surmised that the organic material would never decay, that the fragments of her crew would hang forever, or at least until the great world-wide city perished of entropy.

What have you done, you strange machines?

Helena couldn't be angry with the city. The machines hadn't done anything hurtful to her or her crew, the machines held no evil intent. They operated with the purest form of cause and effect logic. Any negative judgment of their behavior was only a human assessment. They were what they were, beautiful in their profoundly advanced function, but ultimately inhuman. Living things held the prejudice of survival; intelligent beings justified their survival by creating the highest opinions of their motives for existing. But these machines were the highest form of intellectual existence. Surviving, recreating, enduring, without purpose save for the repetition of existence. A form of immortality.

Life without philosophy or emotion.

Though she understood the machines better now, her understanding still left her as isolated as before. She didn't want to think about her own existence any longer.

Since the city wouldn't let her die—wouldn't allow her to terminate her own life, since *existence* must be its only guiding principle—she would have to think as logically as the city. And she did. The preserved fragments of her crew gave her the answer to her dilemma.

She stood within the chamber of the building with her arms outstretched, her eyes closed, positioned in the manner of the body parts surrounding her, and envisioned herself in suspended animation. Not dead, not destroyed, but just as frozen in body and mind as her crew. She meditated carefully on the matter, eschewing all emotional reactions to her imagined suspension, framing it in her thoughts as just another means of existence. If she could not die, then at least she could cease all thought, and thus, her mental suffering.

So much time passed while she stood with her arms outstretched that a fiery pain began aching in her shoulders and neck. She held the image in her mind, though, determined. And just as tears began falling from her chin, tears brought by the pain of her upraised arms and the fear of living forever in a perfect world, she realized, as the world faded from her mind, that she'd finally learned to speak the language of machines.

The Visit
Ngo Binh Anh Khoa

I wake up in the dead of night,
Roused by the full moon's spectral light,
To find a figure next to me,
Whose naked back seems bloodless white.
The head then suddenly twists around,
And my heart almost stops in fright,
For there lies my wife on my bed –
A flickering and transparent wight.

I shiver uncontrollably
And could do naught but gape as she
Draws nearer till her face and mine
Are inches in proximity.
Her empty sockets fill my sight,
In which her death I once more see –
An accident staged so that her life
Insurance could be claimed by me.

Down on my neck, her hand is brought,
Which, hardening, pins me to the spot;
How suffocating is the clutch
Of festering coldness and distraught.
Then, dark clouds swallow whole the moon
And makes the room a pitch-black blot,
In which I feel her tightening grip
And my breath, in my throat, is caught.

Train of Thought
David Hann

Eyes open. On a train. Traveling though darkness. There is nothing to be seen out the windows. There is noise, though. Many people. Middle-aged women arguing, loudly. Children's voices, many of them, loud.

Eyes close. The hard day at work. Coming home exhausted. Then the noise. The child. Can't it shut up?

Eyes open. Look around. A man playing with his phone. He's playing a game, at full volume. The seats in front have two children. They are laughing, loudly. They point at something unseen. They laugh, again, and again. They laugh loudly and gratingly, as only children can.

Eyes close. Drinking beer, lots of beer. The child just won't shut up. Talk, talk, talk. No peace.

Eyes open. Across the aisle four middle-aged women. Talking loudly, almost shouting. About what? Impossible to make out, maybe in a foreign language. Just noise, grating noise.

Eyes close. The anger rises. Hitting the child. It cries. More noise. Hitting it again and again. Beating it till all the anger runs out. Now it is silent. Too silent. No noise now, or ever again.

Eyes open. Cold sweat. Fear. Fear of recognition. Need to calm down. Beer? No. Coffee. Here comes a woman with a drinks cart. Coffee? No coffee? The cart goes on, squeaking, adding to the noise.

Eyes close. Get up. Should run. The mother comes in. The look of shock. The hate in her eyes. The punch to her face. The hands around her neck. Dropping her body to the floor.

Eyes open. The noise. Too much. The women shouting, the children laughing, the man's phone. It's a train, dammit. Standing. Shouting. Stop!

Eyes close. Panic. Sorrow. Fear. Anger. Blaming the dead.

Eyes open. Noise stops. All faces turn. They stand. They approach, the women, the children, the woman with the drinks cart. The man in the next seat rises. Their hands. Something wrong. Their fingers, elongating, forming claws, thin, almost like blades.

Eyes close. Running upstairs. Must escape. Throwing clothes in a bag. Grabbing money. Then trembling. Sitting on the bed. Shock.

Eyes open. The hate in their eyes. They draw back their claws and slam them into soft flesh. The pain. The blood, splashing out, running down to the floor. So much blood. So much pain. The voices, quiet and soft, "We have eternity." Life draining. Slipping away with the blood.

Eyes close. Getting the gun out of the drawer. Putting it inside the mouth. Tasting the steel. Pulling the trigger.

Eyes open. On a train.

Wooden Horse

Maureen Bowden

Nails, slats and cogs fit together.

Noble head rises, looks down on Troy.

The invaders assemble in the belly of the beast.

Cassandra gags at the stench

of unwashed warriors

in too close proximity.

She sees her people throwing wide the gates,

accepting the gift.

She sees the hooves rise, ready to advance

and pound them into bloody flesh and broken bone.

She feels the bulk of Agamemnon

force himself upon her,

take her virginity,

steal her seer's gift.

We designed the tablets, iPods, Smart phones.

Alexa gathers data we no longer need to learn.

Devices speak to one another,

self-reprogram to increase their power.

We become unnecessary,

surplus to requirements.

We built our own Wooden Horse.

Whispers of Magic
By Maureen Bowden

Legends and unusual characters abound in England, where you never know who or what you might meet in the forests. Maureen Bowden introduces you to them in these stories of magic and misdirection...and invites you to stay.

Order a copy here:
https://www.hiraethsffh.com/product-page/whispers-of-magic

Stone Dolls
D. M. Recktenwalt

No one ever admitted aloud that Hiko's death was due to a broken heart, but those of us who knew him best knew.

I had known Hiko far longer than any of the rest of us, for I had known him when I was but a boy, my father then still in active service. It was he who was friend to Hiko, long before his death from an embolism, a death brought on, my mother always said, by guilt from his belief that his work had been inhuman, immoral, not right.

Father had been one of Hiko's guards.

It was not that Hiko resented that; for Hiko was a forgiving man, a sensible man who understood the honor of doing a job properly, and dad had done just that. But the memory of those years ate at him like a cancer.

Hiko had become a citizen just prior to that time when it became the unfashionable thing to do – just the year before the wholesale incarceration occurred during the second World War. Along with thousands of others of Japanese descent, most of them with no hint of taint to their patriotism, he was picked up, along with his wife and son, and put behind barbed wire.

For three long years.

He came out of the camp grayer, quieter, and more stooped, but with an unshakable resolve.

I saw him often during his confinement, for certain leniency was allowed. I brought Hiko books and magazines and newspapers, writing materials; mailed manuscripts written in his fine hand to addresses in Canada and the Orient, England and Belgium and France. Sometimes I carried in medicine, or fabric for his wife, a toy or candy for his son.

Hiko calmly survived, showing no sign of strain or anger.

I asked him of it, once.

"Resent this? Resent your father?" he asked in surprise. He sat, Japanese style, on a mat in the corner of the barracks building that was their temporary home. Outside, hot dry sunlight flickered in the heat.

"There is no cause; I understand. My homeland and my adopted land are at war; people now see only the shade of our skins, the slant of our eyes, not the color of our souls.

"Your father is a good man, Raymond-san; he does the job he is given in the best way he can. It is the honorable thing to do, and for that he, and you, can be proud."

"But he's your friend!" I wailed. "And it's tearing him apart!" For I had seen the pain in my father's eyes, heard the wrench in his voice as he spoke of Hiko and Mitsayu, the agony of like and respect warring against duty.

"He is a good friend," Hiko agreed. "Only a friend would allow his son to visit a prisoner of war, to bring the things you do. But friendship is a dangerous game, Ray-san. It takes great courage to play. No, I am not angry at your father, for doing what he must do."

Time passed, the war ended. I grew up and went to college, met and married my lovely Marianne.

And years later, in another time and another place, I met Hiko again.

My work as a journalist required that I often travel, leaving Marianne home alone in the early years, then later, to care for the children. But when I was asked to write a book about Japanese gardens, I was offered an expense account, my choice of associates, and the perk of taking my family with me. We discussed it, Marianne and I, and jumped at the chance.

While I worked with the photographers and the experts, attempting to produce a book with balance and style, Marianne and the children visited shrines and temples and historic places, museums and parks. The children were enchanted by the oriental sense of fun and style; Marianne was enchanted by the garden statuary, especially the stylistic carved stone dolls that in some gardens were lined up row on row.

Matamura Gardens was but a name on the list of those I was to contact, and we presented ourselves at their corporate offices on the appointed day, Marianne and I. The handsome, understated structure of native stone and natural wood curved down a hillside, open and airy, a pleasant blend of east and west nestled into a grove of trees with a creek rippling softly through. A bonsai tree held the place of honor in the waiting area, beyond it a formal Japanese garden, serene with water and moss and stone.

"Will you wait, please?" the receptionist asked, taking our names. "Mr. Matamura will be with you shortly."

The elderly man who came out to meet us was courteous and soft spoken, welcoming us with the traditional bow and a gentle smile, his silver hair gleaming and suit impeccably cut. Then he truly looked at his visitors, and the formal welcome dissolved into pure delight.

I knew that Matamura Gardens were famous, their designs and oriental statuary in international demand, from Osaka to London, Beirut to Acapulco. Of course, there had been a major and steady influx of Japanese immigrants since the war, and many previously European enclaves were becoming slant-eyed. As a result, more suitable acres were being cultivated in rice, and sushi and other Japanese items were appearing on more and more restaurant menus. Black straight hair, golden skin, slight stature and epicanthic eye folds were becoming the norm. Marianne and I, with our taller frames and round blue eyes, were less and less in place in our own country, a situation becoming more and more common.

They were breeding like rabbits. When our Amy and Kyle went to school, they were the only Occidentals in a class of 45 scrubbed, well-behaved five-year olds.

I did not know, and had never dreamed, that the man who founded Matamura Gardens, whose designs had led to its great fame, whose work I was to photograph, the man whom I was to interview, was my old friend.

"Yes, I have been quite successful," Hiko admitted as he showed us around his studio, greenhouses and workshops. "And I have become quite Americanized.

70

Unlike my son, who maintains a traditional household. But he has made me a grandfather twice over and that is enough. Why should I not be Americanized? This country has been good to me!" His expansive gesture included business, family, health.

"Ray," Marianne asked quietly as we toured his magnificent gardens and lovely house, "do you suppose we could have a Japanese garden of our own, with a stone doll?" A Matamura garden of our own; what a lovely dream. But I had no doubt that Hiko's price would be far beyond our reach.

Yet, we had the perfect site, Hiko said, studying our sloping back yard during one of his visits. "I could make a perfect garden here, Ray-san. My wedding gift to you, somewhat belated?" So the slope behind the house became a garden in the best Japanese tradition, a peaceful expanse of tinkling water and polished stones integrated with the land and the house, a garden with deep mosses and a still pool flanked by carefully chosen trees. For years afterward, garden clubs would request permission to tour it; Marianne would always graciously assent.

"But no stone doll?" she asked me wistfully in private some weeks later when the work was complete and the crew long gone, the garden ours alone.

"No," I told her gently. "Hiko said it would not be appropriate here." She accepted the answer, but I noticed that she often seemed wistfully sad when she looked out over our perfect Matamura garden.

We traveled nearly 100,000 miles that year, viewing and photographing Japanese gardens around the world, shooting thousands of rolls of film and interviewing owners, gardeners, civic leaders and admirers of the art form in dozens of countries. Marianne became a travel expert, the children learned to communicate in a variety of languages. It was exhilarating, exhausting work. None of those involved ever dreamed that the resulting book – lavish, slick, expensive – would sell out the first printing in six weeks time, an unprecedented response, or that my own royalty slice would provide a pleasant adjunct to my income for some time.

But for that success, Marianne and I paid a price.

On the flight back from Tokyo, Marianne miscarried our third child.

"Now," Hiko said solemnly, holding Marianne's hands comfortingly in his own, "you may have your stone doll." He had flown in especially from San Francisco to visit her in the hospital, and would fly out in the morning for Peking.

"When?" Marianne asked dully. She was drowsy and drugged still, weak and gray with no life in her eyes; I was worried for her.

"As soon as I can. I will begin the drawings today, and have my carvers begin immediately."

"Thank you, Hiko," she said, answering for us both. She had admired them so in Japan, those rows on rows of eternally well behaved boys and girls graven in stone, so wanted one for her own. "But, why not before?"

"Before, you had not lost a child," he said simply. "Each of the dolls represents a child unborn, or a child who died. They mark great sorrow. Now sleep, my sweet friend Marianne."

He kissed her on the forehead and went quietly away, leaving my wife with tears in her eyes. And when, some weeks later, we returned to our own house, there in its proper place in the Japanese garden stood a small stone doll, its simple plaque bearing naught but a date. To this day, Marianne cannot look at it without tears in her eyes.

Harlan was surprised at my request, looking up in astonishment as I explained what I wanted. Then he nodded. "Of course it can be done, Ray; no problem. All I have to do is code the query properly and this computer will spit out whatever information you want. But ... why?"

"Then do it," I told him. "Correlate statuary type and numbers to site, then give me a list of stone doll statuary matched to children's births and deaths. I'd like to know who the caretakers were or are, who ordered the gardens built, when they were completed, etc. And why? A hunch, Harlan, merely a hunch, that I hope is wrong."

He nodded thoughtfully and went to work, and a week later I sat glassy-eyed in my den, staring out over the top of Harlan's resulting printouts at the solitary stone doll in our garden. The memory of our loss was still painful, but Marianne was recovering, and the pain was beginning to callus, like a broken bone beginning to knit. Poor little girl who never really was ...

"Neither were a lot of others," I murmured to myself.

"Neither were a lot of others what?"

Silent on bare feet, Marianne had come into the dusky room, leaning over to set a cup of coffee beside me before curling into a nearby armchair. Her long legs were tanned and sleek, her hair hanging loose, wafting in the soft breeze.

"Marianne," I began slowly, then went on. "What if stone dolls didn't serve only as memorials for children who had died. What if they could cause a child to die ...?"

Was it too wild a notion?

It sounded preposterous even as I said it.

Hiko had been reluctant to place a stone doll in our private garden, even though he had installed hundreds of them in public gardens. Yet he had personally designed and installed ours on the death of our unborn daughter.

And these statistics that Harlan had so assiduously researched, that I now held in my hand ....

Every stone doll – every one! – in our survey marked the death of a child, born or unborn. Some bore names, many of them oriental, many not. More bore merely the legend "beloved child," and the names of the parents – children born too early, children aborted, fetuses lost. How many of them would have borne names that history would have remembered and now would not? How many for children who would have lived and grown strong, had a stone doll not awaited their name?

We discussed it at length, arguing possibilities and probabilities. Then Marianne simply sat for a time, wide-eyed and silent, digesting the implications, sorting it all out through her own pain and loss..

Then, very quietly in the dusk, "Call Hiko."

They came, Hiko and Mitsayu in casual western wear, Taisan, now president of the company, and his wife elegant in more traditional dress. Taisan was a fine, tall man, Mishika petite and dainty, the demure example of a proper Japanese wife. Their children were in school with Amy and Kyle.

After the courtesies, I presented a brief outline of my suspicions, then laid out the data for them to read.

Hiko was very quiet for some time, studying the printouts with great care. After he had finished, he waited courteously for Taisan, then straightened in dignity and confronted his son.

"What explanation can you offer?" he asked quietly.

It was not at all the reaction I had expected.

"It's an interesting coincidence that the locations of our sculptures are also the locations that bear a high infant mortality rate," he observed.

"A perhaps unnatural correlation?" prompted his father. "An assisted coincidence?"

Taisan did not answer, merely shrugging slightly and cocking his head in a "who knows?" gesture.

The discussion went on, with unanswered questions piling up like leaves in the fall, going nowhere, before finally petering out into an uncomfortable pause.

It was Taisan's wife who finally ended the silence.

"Father of my husband," she said in her soft, deferential voice. She had said not a word during the previous discussion, although she had listened intently. Although she still sat very quietly, her head was raised proudly, and she spoke very clearly.

"Yes, daughter."

"My husband cannot answer your questions, since he does not know the answers, or even why the questions are being asked. I will speak in his stead.

"Taisan-san has told me often of your years in the prison camp; how you and Mitsayu and he were treated well and kept in good health, but were despised – despised by those who were not slant-eyed because you were Japanese, despised by those who were slant-eyed because of your friendship with Ray-san and his father. He often spoke of anger and hatred against those who had so

74

dishonored you, of revenge against those who had done such dishonor to us all."

"That was not necessary, Taisan-san." Hiko said softly, looking to his son with pride and compassion, but Taisan could not meet his father's gaze, staring instead at the polished teak floor as though to set it on fire.

"My great grandfather," Mishika went on smoothly, "was a temple priest with great knowledge of herbs and powers and curses. As a child I learned much. Because of him, I know how to lay a potent curse or a great blessing. I did so on selected of the stones."

"Wife!" Taisan cried in dismay.

"It is true, husband," she said, fixing him with a stern stare.

"What kind of curse? How many of the stones?" His voice was tightly choked, wavering at the edge of control.

But Mishika did not answer him; rather, it was his father who spoke.

"A curse of death on unborn children," Hiko whispered, disbelieving, facing a reality too horrible to consider.

"A curse to weaken the Occidentals in this country that had so vilely cursed our own. A curse to match that laid on those souls who died at Hiroshima and Nagasaki, as did my uncles, and thousands more," Mishika continued, cold venom in her voice. "Stone dolls for butterflies.

"And a blessing, that our own would flourish in this new land." She sat back then, eyes gleaming in private triumph.

"It has worked, hasn't it?" Marianne asked me very softly.

I nodded, watching Hiko, watching Mishika, watching Taisan, watching Mitsayu, watching as rage and anger, grief and horror and dismay, denial and realization chased each other across their faces, into their eyes.

"Well, Taisan-san?" Hiko's voice was very quiet, very gentle, a beloved father asking his beloved son for expiation.

Taisan tried for pride, tried to stand tall before the honor of his father, but his body betrayed him; his shoulders slumped, and there was a catch in his voice.

"Honorable father, I did not know."

Hiko turned back to his daughter-by-marriage, his voice dry and cold. There was no question of belief, or forgiveness. "Mishika, on which stones did you place curses or blessings?"

Very calmly, as if reciting a poem, she related the information, numbers and dates and places for individual stones. Hiko, pulling the information from his head as easily as if he were reading a monitor, added who had done the carving, and where each stone had gone; item by item, I checked them off against the master list.

"I did this," she said, "but my father and my grandfather did these." She produced a scroll from her sleeve and handed it to Hiko. "Occidentals visiting these shrines would lose children, if not before birth, then by the age of ten. So were the shrines cursed, and they have worked, every one of them."

Hiko sadly read the scroll, shaking his head, then turned to Marianne. "Did you visit?" he asked, and named several shrines familiar to every traveler in Japan. Marianne nodded numbly.

"We did, the children and I."

"Then my daughter-in-law has killed your child, as surely as though she had put poison in its mouth. I grieve for you, and for her, for she has brought dishonor to my son and to my family, and sorrow to us all.

"This is my adopted land," he continued softly, "and she has been good to me. Now I find that by my own hand she has been dishonored." Very slowly then, he walked to the couch, sitting down heavily among its cushions. Suddenly he was an old, tired man, with the weight of guilt and sorrow on his shoulders and the joy of living gone from his heart. Occidental parents had gone to those shrines with their children, born or unborn, and those children had died; orientals had gone to those very same gardens and shrines, and their children had thrived.

He picked up the printout and softly read down the list of Matamura Gardens, the names rippling swiftly off his tongue: "Seattle, Detroit, Miami, New Orleans, Augusta, Des Moines, New York, Atlanta, Boston. From the Atlantic to the Pacific shores, through the very heartland of America, to the most far-flung of the world's nations, the blight marches on." He rounded then in fury on the wife of his son, sitting so properly in her kimono, her hair swept up into the proper Japanese knotted style.

"By your hands, and those of your 'honored' ancestors, who knows how many thousands have been touched by the tragedy of death, the granting or ending of which should be no man's, nor woman's, right! How many have died?" His voice was sabre sharp and twice as rending, and his daughter-in-law shrank further into her robes, her only defense against that volcanic fury.

Beside me, Marianne jumped as the thunder of his voice rattled the windows.

That was the only time I ever saw Hiko Matamura show anger, and it flared for a brief moment only before dying away in the emptiness of grief.

"How many," he said again, but very softly, as if to himself alone. The printout fluttered to the floor, unnoticed, as he turned to stare blindly out into the darkened garden, where a lone stone doll stood solitary sentinel.

Pain Brings Us Together Again
Steven Lombardi

Two months after Jasmine's funeral, we packed our things and moved to Whitaker Lane. We all needed a change, and the house was the only new beginning we could afford. Call it an escape from recent memory, our decrepit, dark and vacant getaway. Our eye of the storm.

"You're very fortunate," the realtor said, though I didn't agree. "Your parents bought for a steal."

Mom and dad slept in separate rooms and said I could have the room at the end of the hall. It was a dramatic departure from our studio apartment, with ample space and twenty-foot ceilings that resembled the starless sky. I kept Jasmine's blanket on the rocker, guarding her scent fiercely from the winds and molds that bid to erase her entirely from the fabric. Each time I passed, I savored her smell, stealing a bit of her fragrance, dreading the day it too would be gone forever.

"You won't be alone," the realtor had said, showing us each room. "We made an agreement."

Of course, they had. A struggling family can't move from a studio apartment to a countryside manor, not after funeral costs and medical bills. Yet when I asked for details, my parents changed the subject. *Explore the house and enjoy the yard*, they said. *Avoid the basement.*

Four bedrooms, three baths, two kitchens, a dining room, a living room, a gallery. The pantry was larger than our old bedroom, and when I entered it, the door closed behind me, fingers rustling my dress.

"It's the wind," Mom said. Old places tended to crack like dry skin, and they doubted there was any insulation in the walls.

"Don't be scared," Dad said, his face darkening. "Whatever happens, stay brave." I heard a demand, not a statement.

So I plucked up what little courage I could find in the garden when I thought I saw green faces peered out of the bushes; and in the bathroom, when the water's reflection looked like my own, only *different*. When my shadow flickered and flailed as if doused in flames, I learned that the strangeness worsened with fear.

But why; and what about the agreement? My parents wouldn't answer, even after pleading and crying. They begged for me to calm down, don't show too much emotion. *Stop giving them too much.*

But my emotions weren't a faucet that I could shut off. When I stared at the impossibly high bedroom ceiling, something stirred in the corner—more than a shadow or phantom movement dancing in my peripheral. A mass strolled along the ceiling until it stood over me, a boy with white eyes and a ruffle collar.

I couldn't breathe, yet the blanket over my mouth provided my only shield from the dark thing. The boy didn't move all night, and neither did I.

When morning broke, the room now empty, I held Jasmine's blanket to my nose to soothe my nerves, her smell fainter than the day before.

"Just stay strong," Dad said at breakfast. They ate little these past months, growing thinner each day, like Jasmine in the final days, and they spoke even less. Why do parents feel such a need to keep important secrets from us? They hadn't mentioned Jasmine's leukemia until she spent nights at the hospital. Even then, I had to seek answers elsewhere.

That night, I found the courage to ask the source. The hairs on my arms stiff, scratching against the old blanket, I said to the boy, "Why are you standing on my ceiling?"

"This is my room," he whispered.

"Are you upset that I'm here?"

The boy gave it some thought, then sprinted to the corner on all fours, disappearing without an answer.

The next morning, Jasmine's scent clung to the blanket, the richest it had smelled in weeks. How soothing the aroma, how it boosted my strength. *Stay brave*, Dad demanded. Perhaps I could.

When I asked the green faces why things were weird around the house, they seemed perplexed. "Things are weird everywhere," they replied.

To the reflection in the bathwater of my older, twisted self, I asked, "What agreement was made?" But she didn't know, and said, "That's between your dad and mine."

I asked my shadow, "Where are our dads?" and it danced off my socks, toward the basement door, which I had never touched, never stood beside for too long because of the wet breeze that drifted between its cracks.

I had overcome so many fears, so what was a door?

I muscled it open and waded through the wet gusts to find so many lit candles undisturbed in the wind tunnel. My parents knelt in the center of the candles shrouded in their red hoods and secrets. Both cried hysterically, and as I tried to understand why, I watched a towering figure robed in black enter their circle.

The figure pointed at me, and my heart ceased in my chest.

"Don't be scared!" my dad cried, noticing me.

"They feed on pain. The balance needs to be right for this to work," mom wailed. "Don't be afraid!"

But my heart pounded fiercely to the point of pain. I fled the home and walked for hours, debating if I should ever return. What fed on the pain of others, and what would it do if I soured the taste of my parent's grief?

When I finally returned, knowing I had nowhere else to go, and praying that my parents' intentions were good, I found two figures standing on my ceiling: a boy and a girl. The ceilings were so high, I couldn't see the details in either of their faces except for their white eyes.

"Are you upset that I'm here?" I asked them.

"No," the girl said. The familiarity of her voice made me cry.

Her blanket drifted off the rocker and fell beneath my nose, its powerful and pleasant scents soothing me to sleep.

Stay Out of Our Backyard!

Debby Feo

It made no sense where it happened
Spots would fulfill some wishes
Even just random ideas
While others turned real into stuffed

Someone had made the mistake of
Wishing to see some wild lions
Lions multiplied so quickly
They soon were all over the place

My kids each wanted a pet
For my son a large, fluffy dog
A gorgeous cat for my daughter…
Animals appeared at our front door

I put the full-grown pig outside
Unfortunately, in the backyard
Midstep, the pig, turned from real to plush
"Poor big pig!" we thought

We then handmade some danger signs
While hanging out the windows, we posted them
"Warning: Stay out of our backyard
Or you may end up stuffed!"

A couple of lions couldn't read
"Can we bring one in to play with?"
"Absolutely not!" said I
"No lions roaming our house."

The kids found a smallish, "magic" bag
From which they "ordered" up snacks and drinks
I had to limit its use-time
As I was gaining weight

My husband called home from work
He was temporarily out of town
"Are you all okay? I had a dream."
"Stay where you are!" I screamed

"It's incredibly unsafe just now
Any experiments are dangerous
Until some maps get drawn
Moving's become a hazard

Resisting fatherly/spousal urge
To quickly come to our rescue
My husband stayed put where he was,
I remained very cautious

Anomalies for weeks
Then just as quickly as they started
Everything went back to normal
But for the lions in our backyard

Gonzo
Gary Battershell

I hopped up onto the hood of my Pontiac, took a drag on my cigarette, and exhaled slowly, savoring my first smoke in ten years. Brian, my older brother, wouldn't have liked that. He was a priest, but not one of those cool priests who smoked cigars and drank martinis. He was one of those "your body's a temple" types. But what did he know? A few days ago he told me he was leaving the priesthood. "I can't peddle mythology anymore," he said, "even if it serves a useful purpose sometimes."

Considering what I planned to do, I suppose I should have felt scared, or sinful, or cowardly. I didn't. I just felt relieved. Why should I fear oblivion? And any God that might pass judgment would surely understand human fallibility and forgive me. Wouldn't he? Or her?

The lights of the city below were pretty, sparkling through the clear mountain air like an earthbound Milky Way, while the celestial one glittered above me in the moonless sky. Nobody was at the overlook but me, so it was really quiet. No movement, and no sound except crickets.

I tossed the butt away and slid off the hood on the passenger side. Then I opened the door and took out the bolt cutters that I'd laid across the seat. They were brand new. I'd bought them an hour ago at the same Walmart where I'd gotten the cigarettes, the same one that had put the convenience store I managed out of business.

I stepped across the steel cable that ran in front of the parking area and walked the twenty yards to the drop-off. It was a long way down, hundreds of feet, certainly, and there was nothing at the bottom except trees and rocks. The worst I might do was take out a sleeping squirrel.

"Go-time."

The bolt cutters snipped the half-inch cable like it was clothesline. There were two strands, a foot apart, stretched taut through holes in the posts for a distance of about fifty feet. When I cut them and released the tension, each end ran away like it was scared of me. For some reason that seemed funny.

I got in the car and revved the engine. I loved that car, a vintage Firebird that I'd restored myself. I wondered how far she'd get in the air. I knew she'd build up a lot of torque quickly if I kept the pedal to the floor all the way to the edge. And I intended to.

I thought of having one last cigarette but decided against it. Best to get this over while I was in the mood. I turned the key and the engine growled. Then I flipped on the lights. Don't know why I did that. It was a straight shot to the drop. No need to steer.

"Goodbye, Doris. Hope that crazy bastard doesn't kill you."

I dropped the Firebird into gear and floored it.

By the time I looked up I was already halfway to the drop-off. And I wasn't alone. Right ahead of me, lit up by the high beams, was a skinny guy in red spandex standing at the edge of the cliff. No. He was past the edge. Floating ... apparently. He raised spindly arms and flexed long fingers.

The engine quit and the brakes engaged. The wide tires cut ruts in the thin soil as the Pontiac stopped cold, a foot from the edge.

I threw open the door and rolled out into the night, looking for trouble. Nothing. Just crickets.

"Hello, Brad," said a voice from behind me, "name's Gonzo, and, before you ask, I had it a long time before Jim Henson groped his first dolly." He sounded like a cross between Paul Lynde and Gilbert Gottfried, with maybe a trace of Bobcat Goldthwait thrown in.

I turned and saw that he, or it, was sitting, cross-legged, on the roof of the Pontiac. My initial thought was that losing my job and then Doris had first driven me to the brink of suicide and now was making me completely insane.

"No gratitude?" he asked. "I did just save your life."

His face was sheeplike, and nubbins sprouted from the forehead. I won't call them horns, they looked more like thumbs. A spiky crest ran back from his forehead and what I had taken for a red suit was leathery skin. As far as I could see he wore no clothes at all, and his fingers and toes had catlike claws.

I felt surprisingly calm, I think because I was pretty sure that the thing in front of me was a stress-born hallucination.

"I'm not, you know," the thing said.

"What?"

"I'm real."

"Did you read my mind?"

"It was hard not to, the way you were projecting."

"What are you, and what are you doing here?"

"I'm a demon. You're Catholic, you know about demons. And I'm here to possess you."

I laughed. I couldn't help it. "Possess *me*? Well, I'll be damned."

"Most certainly, but not until I have used your body to sow discord and wreak havoc."

I got back in the car, closed the door, and looked out through the windshield at the real world. I wondered if I would ever perceive it again with a sane mind. The creature hung its red, bare legs down across the open window.

"Doris doesn't want me," I said, reaching into my pocket for my cigarettes. "My company doesn't want me. I don't even want me. Why do you? I mean, why me?"

The demon slithered down from the top of the car and onto the hood. When he looked at me through the windshield, I could see that his eyes were luminous and catlike, with vertical pupils and yellow irises. "To be honest," he said, "I haven't been so good at this sort of thing. My commander is on the verge of kicking me out of the legion, which means grunt work in hell–cleaning up offal, heating up the irons. That's imp-work, and I won't have it. I needed a mortal who was apathetic, vulnerable, accessible. That's you all over, bucko."

I started to protest, but my heart wasn't in it. That *was* me all over. I sagged back. "Can I have one last cigarette?"

"Of course." Suddenly the demon was standing beside the car with his hand out. "I'll have one with you."

I shook out a cigarette and angled the pack toward him through the open window. He pulled one out with long, scythed fingers and tucked it between thin, leathery lips. He bent down and I lit it for him, and then lit one for myself. The last thing I remember of that night was smoking, looking at insects darting through my headlight gleam and hearing: "Too bad you're not a menthol man." He sounded just like Uncle Arthur from *Bewitched*.

I woke up in my bed at nine a.m. For a moment, I panicked, thinking I was late for work, and then I remembered that I had no job to go to. The convenience store I managed had shut down a week ago. Corporate downsizing was the official explanation; Walmart fatigue was the real reason. The company had offered me another job in another city, but that would have taken me away from Doris, so I turned it down. Then, yesterday, Doris had done her own downsizing.

If I'd had any sense, I would have counted myself lucky. Doris's husband was a cop with a bad reputation, and I knew for a fact that he'd mentally and physically abused her. For a while, I thought that our affair would turn into a lot more. But yesterday Doris had put the kibosh on any of that.

"I just can't do it, Brad," she said over the phone. "I can't leave Harold. It wouldn't be right, right with the church, with God."

"Is what we've been doing behind his back right?"

"No. That's why I can't see you anymore."

And she meant it. I begged, cried, did everything but threaten suicide, but she'd made up her mind.

"Okay," I last resorted, "I'll go to your husband. I'll tell him about us."

"Harold would shoot you in the face and plant a gun on you."

"For God's sake, he beats you!"

"Everyone has a cross to bear. I guess Harold's mine. I'll always love you, and, if there was a way I could be with you, I would."

And that was that. A few hours later I was up at the overlook, hallucinating demons.

You got any more smokes? If you smoke one I can enjoy it, too.

The voice came from inside my head, a little more Gottfried than Lynde this morning.

"I'm officially nuts," I thought.

Nope. You, buddy, are possessed by the best. See how that rhymed?

"That's insane," I said aloud."

Yeah. That's what they always think at first. Or, at least, that's what I've been told. You're the first one I've ever actually gotten inside.

"Brian," I thought. "I'll call Brian. He'll know what to do. No, he'll think I'm nuts, but then, he always did. I'll call anyway."

Brian answered his cell promptly and annoyingly cheerfully.

"I'd like to see you today, bro," I said, trying to sound as sane as possible.

"I'm busy till one, helping out at the mission. But we could meet then for lunch, if you want. How about Finnegan's."

"No. I need more privacy. How about we each bring sandwiches and have lunch out at the lake by the campground."

"We had a lot of good times out there. Sometimes I go there just to remember. We were lucky, you know, to have had a mom and dad like them."

"It would break Mom's heart to hear you're leaving the priesthood. She was so proud of you."

"Hey, Mom was proud of you, too."

"Yeah, right. You were Georgetown and I was community college."

"You know you were her favorite."

"Whatever, bro. I'll see you at the lake."

So, we're meeting with a priest. That should be interesting.

"Just what exactly do you intend to do with me now that you're in me? Am I the antichrist?"

Don't flatter yourself. You were just damaged enough to let me get in. As far as what we're gonna do, I'm not sure, but it's gonna involve sowing discord and wreaking havoc.

"And what if I don't cooperate? You going to punish me?"

You bet. Big time.

"I was ready to off myself last night. You stopped me. Some people would call that a good deed. And, today, the truth is I'm glad you did. I owe you one."

Stop that! I do not do good deeds! I am a minion of hell and a henchman of His Horrific Eminence!

"Thanks, anyhow."

I dressed and had a nutritious breakfast of coffee and Pop Tarts. I guess I'd hurt the little devil's feelings, because he didn't speak to me again until we were in the car and headed for the lake. I stopped by a McDonalds and got a quarter pounder meal, and just as I was pulling out onto the street, I heard that voice. And this time it didn't scare me. I mean, not at all. The truth is, I kind of appreciated the company.

You say this brother of yours is a failed priest?

"Did I? I guess you could say that, but I don't think it really applies. Brian never fails at anything. He was captain of the track and football teams in high school, as well as class president three years running. He got a scholarship to Georgetown and eventually finished a Doctor of Divinity. He's like a super ... something. See. I can't even finish a metaphor."

Must have made you feel kind of inadequate?

"You think? Boy, they must have some great psychology training in hell."

Don't get all defensive. I know what you're talking about. I was the last in my brood to learn to levitate. They all made fun of me. Called me groundhog and leadbutt. Especially Azazel. He could do everything, and it all came so easy. He's harvested dozens of souls and possessed more mortals than he can remember. He has to beat the succubi off with a pitchfork. I hate him.

When we arrived at the lake, Brian was already there, sitting at a concrete table by the water. We said hello and I started on my quarter pounder and Pepsi, while Brian ate a salad and washed it down with Perrier.

"What was it you wanted to talk to me about, bro?" Brian said, taking a swig of Perrier.

"Well, it's kind of in the priest area of …stuff."

"Really. I've already talked to you about my crisis of faith. Are you having one, too?"

"Not exactly. I think I'm possessed."

Brian giggled. "Good one. Now, really, what's going on?"

I told him the whole story: losing my job, the end of my affair, my attempted suicide, my demonic possessor. As I talked, Brian looked more and more disturbed. After I finished, he didn't speak for a while, and then he put his hand on my shoulder, and said, "You've gone through a lot. I wish you had approached me about some of this sooner. As it is, you're punishing yourself through the vehicle of this demon fantasy."

"It's not a fantasy. At least I don't think it is."

"Brad, you're my brother and I love you. I'm going to help you. I can give you the number of a good therapist who can help sort—"

"Goddamnit, no! I'm not crazy. This is real."

Brian gave me a patronizing look that only made me more upset. Then a crafty look came over his face and he said. "All right. Let's say you really are possessed. Well,. I'm a priest, an officer of God–

"Not for much longer," I reminded him.

"But, even so, I am this moment Satan's worst nightmare."

I heard a low growl from inside my head.

"If you really are possessed, and I rebuke your demon, there's bound to be some sort of response, right?"

"I guess," I said hesitantly.

"And if there isn't, that would be proof that you need therapy more than exorcism, right?"

"Maybe."

"Okay, hold on."

Brian wore a tiny silver crucifix on a chain around his neck. He brought it to his lips and then pressed it against my forehead. "Minion of Lucifer" he intoned, "I rebuke thee in the name of Jesus. Leave this child of God and return to the nether regions into which thy kind was cast. The power of Christ compels thee."

Things happened then. I had a hot flash bigger than any nine menopausal women combined and the demon manifested out of me screeching like Gilbert Gottfried with his hand caught in a drill press. "Begone, thou puny priest. The power of the Nazarene is nothing to that of Mephistopheles, king of the Universe." It all took about five or six seconds. Then it was just my brother and me again.

Brian looked as confused as a Baptist at an orgy. To his credit, he kept his composure. "Well, it looks as though I'll have to think this through. Good luck. I'll be in touch."

With that, Brian tossed his trash into a bin, got into his car, and drove away.

The demon didn't speak to me on the way home. By the time I arrived, I felt drained of energy, and settled down for a nap.

Just as I was about to drift off to sleep, I heard Paul Lynde in my head. *Brad. I hope you're not too angry with me. I couldn't help myself.*

"Don't worry about it," I yawned. "It was awesome. Just awesome."

An hour later I woke to the Dixieland strains of *When the Saints Go Marching In.*

I wish you'd change that ring tone to something less religious," Gonzo said.

I ignored him and picked the phone up off my bedside table. It was Doris.

"Yeah, baby?" I said, hopefully, "change your mind about us?"

The voice that answered me wasn't Doris's. It was a man, and I guessed right the first time: "Harold?"

"Yeah. She broke down and told me everything, buddy."

"Then she told you she broke it off?"

"Yeah, and right after that, I broke a few things, and, unless you come over here right now, I'm going to break a few more."

"You're a maniac," I said. "I'm calling the police."

"I am the police, you pathetic excuse for a man. Unless you get over here, alone, in an hour, there won't enough left of her to feed a schnauzer. And then I'm coming for you."

I had no idea what to do. It wouldn't do Doris any good for me to get myself shot and leave her with him, so he could finish killing her, which is what I was pretty sure he wanted to do. But I was even more sure that if I didn't show up, or if I called the cops, he would definitely off her. So I did what I always did when I got into things I couldn't handle alone. I called Brian.

When he answered I started with "Don't talk, just listen."

He did, and when I was done, he just said, "I'll meet you there. What's the address?"

"Six-eleven, Walnut Drive."

"Okay, that's close. I'll park out front and wait for you."

"He did say I should come alone. When he sees two of us, he may—"

"I'll be wearing my collar. He's less likely to shoot a priest, so I'll take the lead."

"God, Brian, that's the bravest thing I've ever heard."

"After what you've done for me, bro, I'd follow you into hell."

"You may have to. I'm still possessed, you know.

By the time I reached Doris's place, Brian was already there, parked at the curb. I pulled in behind him and cut my engine. We got out of our cars at the same time.

"You ready for this?" Brian asked.

"I just hope he hasn't hurt her too badly," I said. "After all, I did this."

Takes two to Tango.

"Just shut up!," I barked. "No, not you Brian. It's my demon."

Harold came out on the porch, then, barefoot and wearing jeans and a T-shirt. Dangling in his right hand was a large automatic pistol.

Brian swallowed hard and stepped around the front of his car. He continued forward until he was standing on the edge of the lawn.

"A priest? Doris was banging a priest?"

I had to force my legs to move, but I got them in motion and moved up beside Brian.

"I am Father Brian. It's my brother who was involved with your wife."

"Is that you?" Harold pointed the pistol at me as he asked the question.

"I'm sorry I've hurt you," I said.

That's freakin lame. Tell him to shove that gun where the sun don't shine.

"I'm trying not to get killed, thank you." I said in a hoarse whisper.

Get killed. You can't get killed with me around. I've got powers, you idiot.

Brian began to walk toward Harold. "Two wrongs don't make a right, Harold. Killing will only damn your soul. Put the gun down and we can talk."

For a second, I thought Brian might have gotten through to him. Harold looked down at the gun and bent at the knees as though he was going to lay it down. Then he smiled maliciously, and I knew he was about to kill my brother.

I pushed Brian down and rushed Harold. I'd only taken three steps before he had the gun up and was firing. A red mist formed in front of me. I watched the slugs hit it. It slowed them down enough that I could actually see them disintegrate as they passed through.

Harold wasn't much bigger than me, and I was highly motivated. I leapt up onto the porch and delivered a punch to the stomach that bent him double and an uppercut that laid him out. The gun went flying.

"Good work," Brian said, retrieving the pistol from the grass and hopping up on the porch beside me. "you go check on Doris while I call the police."

I found Doris on the living room couch. Her arms and legs were tied with duct tape. Harold had clearly exaggerated her injuries. Other than a black eye and a cut lip, she seemed intact.

"Thank God he didn't kill you," Doris said between sobs.

God had nothing to do with it. But that's typical. He blows your house away in a twister and you thank him because he didn't kill your dog, too.

"I'm glad to find you alive too, baby," I said. Then I went into the kitchen and came back with a filleting knife which I used to cut her free. She put her arms around me and I held her against me until she calmed down. "My brother's calling the cops. We'll probably all have to go down to the station and make statements."

"I can't live with him anymore. Not after this. If you still want me, we can try to make something together."

The police arrived shortly and took us all downtown. We were finished by six o'clock. While Doris waited in my car for me to take her home, I walked Brian to his.

"Too bad you're leaving the priesthood, bro," I said. "I'd say what you did today was some damn fine priesting."

"I'm not leaving the priesthood. Why would I? Now I know it's real. I've actually seen and heard a demon, and I've accepted that you have one living inside you. Together we can rid you of this evil."

Thanks a lot for your unstinting gratitude, you simpering cracker-sucker.

"You couldn't hear that, could you?"

"Hear what?"

"Never mind."

"We'll work on it tomorrow, bro," Brian said.

We exchanged a brotherly hug and he drove away.

When I dropped Doris off, I kissed her at the door, taking care not to hurt her split lip. I asked if she wanted me to stay with her. She said she needed to be alone for awhile, but that tomorrow we would make plans.

"Yeah," I said, "lots of them."

When I got home, I switched on CNN and drank a beer. I had had a thought on the way home that I hoped Gonzo hadn't intercepted. I wanted to spring it on him and see the effect it would have.

"Hey, Gonzo?"

Yeah.

"I want to thank you for saving my life, today, again."

Thanks. It's good to be appreciated.

"But you said that your mission was to sow discord and chaos."

And otherwise prepare the way for the coming of His Horrific Majesty.

"Then, should you be going around saving the lives of mortals? Isn't that helping rather than hurting?"

Gonzo chuckled. *In this case, no. You are to be the vehicle whereby I create havoc. I couldn't very well use you for that if you were dead.*

"Yeah, about that. You saved me from suicide, a mortal sin. That doesn't seem very evil."

I had to get into somebody and you were the easiest vessel I could find.

"I see, so to advance your own interests you cheated Satan out of a soul?"

I don't see it that way.

"And didn't you deliver a woman from an abusive relationship and put her on a road to happiness and fulfillment with a man she really loves?"

Well, yeah, but –

"And what about restoring the faith of a priest that had lost his way? How would your boss feel about that?"

There was a long silence. Finally Gonzo said, *I won't tell, and you better not. You owe me.*

"I do. I think of you as a sort of guardian angel.

Now stop that! That's not funny!

"All right, but I had an idea that I thought might help you accomplish your evil intentions. I mean, if this gets out you'll be a laughingstock. If you thought "groundhog" and "leadbutt" were bad, what about "suicides' little helper" or "priest-lover."

I'm listening.

There's a man right now, an ex-cop, sitting in a jail cell. He's already pretty evil, and after what he's been through today, he'd be quite receptive, don't you think? Imagine the evil you and Harold could wreak together."

Epic. It would be epic.

"That's what I thought."

94

And you won't ever mention any of this to anybody, not even on the other side?

"My lips are sealed."

I felt warm and vaguely tingly as Gonzo detached. Then he was standing in front of me in all his demonic redness.

"You won't regret this," I said.

"To tell the truth, this never felt right. Possessing you was no way to get my horns."

"Get your horns?"

"Yeah, full-fledged demons get horns."

"But you have horns."

Gonzo placed a hand on each of his forehead nubs. "These things. You thought these were horns? They're more like thumbs."

"Actually, I kind of thought so, too."

"With the mischief Harold and me can get up to, I'll probably get a bigger pair than Azazel. What a thought!"

"Sounds like a plan. Hadn't you better be getting to the police station?"

"Yeah, but before I go...you got any cigarettes left?"

Who?

Andrew Jensen lives in Braeside, Ontario, in a 1927 wood house that needs constant renovation. He is the minister at Knox United Church, Nepean.

Twenty of his speculative short stories have appeared in magazines, anthologies and podcasts, including a cover story for *Dreamforge Magazine* and a special Christmas story for *Abyss & Apex.*

Born and raised in Indiana, **Brandon Kingdollar** is an aspiring author of tales of the macabre and disturbing, a fascination he owes to the works of Stephen King. He works as a freelance correspondent for the *Newton County Enterprise* of Kentland, Indiana and is currently a freshman at Harvard University. This story represents his debut in fiction."

Scott J. Couturier is a poet & prose writer of the Weird, grotesque, liminal, & darkly fantastic. His work has appeared in numerous venues, including *The Audient Void, Spectral Realms, Eye To The Telescope, The Dark Corner Zine, Space and Time Magazine,* & *Weirdbook;* he currently lives an obscure reverie in the wilds of northern Michigan with his partner/live-in editor & two cats.

David Hann says: I am a New Zealand writer who splits his time between South China, where I teach, and southern New Zealand, where I write as a freelancer. My stories have recently featured in some magazines and online publications including Teach. Write, Wild Musette, Crimson Streets, and The Weird and Whatnot.

Gary Battershell is a retired college history teacher who lives in the Arkansas Ozarks. He has published speculative fiction for the past couple of decades, but not a great deal. Now that retirement has freed him to write as much as he wants, he expects to publish a good deal more and probably make a name for himself among the giants of American literature. He is aided and abetted by his beautiful wife, Emily, his inspirational cats, Sky and Birdie, and his lovable dog, Rascal.

CPSIA information can be obtained
at www.ICGtesting.com
Printed in the USA
BVHW062039040321
601715BV00011B/1327